***"I came over early to drive you to work," Paul said.***

"There's nothing wrong with walking," Kathy said. "It's excellent exercise for the heart."

"So is this." He drew her into his arms, and the kiss he gave her was as soft as the morning, without force, without demand. Yet inside her, desire stirred. It seemed entirely natural to lean against him, to let him support her weight, to concentrate on the kiss.

His fingers wove through her hair and tightened. "I like your hair loose," he murmured, then kissed her again, harder, deeper, until she was breathless in his arms.

Delicious. With a little more of this she could become addicted. And if that happened, it would be very hard to ever get enough of his kisses to feel satisfied. . . .

**WHAT ARE *LOVESWEPT* ROMANCES?**

They are stories of true romance and touching emotion. We believe those two very important ingredients are constants in our highly sensual and very believable stories in the *LOVESWEPT* line. Our goal is to give you, the reader, stories of consistently high quality that may sometimes make you laugh, sometimes make you cry, but are always fresh and creative and contain many delightful surprises within their pages.

Most romance fans read an enormous number of books. Those they truly love, they keep. Others may be traded with friends and soon forgotten. We hope that each *LOVESWEPT* romance will be a treasure—a "keeper." We will always try to publish

*LOVE STORIES YOU'LL NEVER FORGET*
*BY AUTHORS YOU'LL ALWAYS REMEMBER*

The Editors

LOVESWEPT® • 284

# Fayrene Preston

# Emerald Sunshine

BANTAM BOOKS
TORONTO • NEW YORK • LONDON • SYDNEY • AUCKLAND

*EMERALD SUNSHINE*
*A Bantam Book / October 1988*



ISBN 0-553-21913-8

*Published simultaneously in the United States and Canada*

---

*Bantam Books are published by Bantam Books, a division of Bantam Doubleday Dell Publishing Group, Inc. Its trademark, consisting of the words "Bantam Books" and the portrayal of a rooster, is Registered in U.S. Patent and Trademark Office and in other countries. Marca Registrada. Bantam Books, 666 Fifth Avenue, New York, New York 10103.*

---

PRINTED IN THE UNITED STATES OF AMERICA

O 0 9 8 7 6 5 4 3 2 1

*To Kay Garteiser*

*Thank you for being one terrific lady,
and for not once over the years
letting me forget about Paul.*

# One

The weather was too nice for the first part of December, Kathy thought, pedaling her bicycle along the street. The constant sunshine and seventy-degree temperature of the past few days were really getting to be annoying. And this morning, the weather forecaster had cheerfully stated that the temperature in Dallas would remain above normal for the next five days.

"Bah, humbug!" Kathy muttered. At this rate, it would take a miracle to get a white Christmas.

As she wheeled her bicycle around the corner and onto the street which led to Bluebonnet Village, she decided that she'd have to readjust her thinking. As a New Englander who had moved to Texas within the last year, she'd have to learn to live without snow. She could do it. After all, millions did it every year. She just wondered *how* they did it, that was all.

Hunger gnawed at her stomach, making her remember that she'd left home without eating. Normally she had at least toast for breakfast, but this morning she'd managed to burn her last piece of bread. And it had been a heel at that! Her grip on the handle bars tightened. She was used to being a little hungry, she reminded herself. She wasn't bothered at all. And after everything was said and done, food was the least of her worries.

She looked at the neat bungalows she was passing; pine wreaths with big, red floppy bows hung on doors, and occasionally she caught a glimpse of a Christmas tree. That was good, she thought. People were getting into the holiday spirit early. Now if only that spirit would prompt new customers to come into her crafts shop. She desperately needed the business! The shop wasn't close to making a profit yet, and her normally optimistic nature was beginning to fray at the edges.

She was willing to work hard, to sacrifice to make the shop successful. She'd known it was going to be difficult because she'd studied the dismal statistics on the failure rate for new businesses.

In the last seven months she'd been at her most creative in figuring out how to make a dollar bill go ten different ways. She'd been at her least creative in finding time to make new friends. And so, added to her business woes was loneliness. She sorely missed her home, her friends, and her family back in Connecticut. And now she was yearning for the one thing she never thought she'd miss: snow.

Since Kathy had been in Dallas, she'd grown to

like the area. Really like it. But this time of year there should be snow. Everyone knew that. It was *winter*, for heaven's sake!

She raised her head and glowered at the clear, blue sky. Where was the *snow*?

In the next instant, her bicycle collided with a wall that had obviously been constructed overnight, and in the middle of the street too! As she catapulted off her bicycle, then flew forward, she could only think, *How odd*. Her forehead struck something sharp and hurtful, her body toppled . . . and she fell right into a pair of strong arms.

"Are you hurt?" a deep voice asked. The voice slid sideways, or seemed to, and so did her body.

"No." Kathy reluctantly opened her eyes and gazed around. How bewildering, she thought. Luxury. Rich leather. A phone and a TV. Like Alice in Wonderland, she found that her free-fall through space had made her lose touch with reality. Alice had had her rabbit hole, but Kathy had fallen into a limousine. And she was sitting on the lap of one of the best-looking men she'd ever seen in her life.

Dazed, she wasn't sure whether the wonderfully masculine scent was coming from the man or from the plush interior of the limousine. The scent seemed a mixture of spice, lime, and leather, and she decided it was definitely the cause of her lightheaded feeling.

Noticing that the wonderfully handsome man was staring at her with a worried expression on his marvelous face, she asked, "What happened?"

"I'm afraid it was all my fault. I opened the door without checking first to see if anyone was coming. And you ran right into it."

"I was looking at the sky," she murmured, transfixed by his eyes. They were blue with glints of gray, and for some reason, she found those glints of gray extraordinarily interesting. "It's not snowing."

"No, it's not," he said in the gentle tone one uses with those who are not quite right in the head.

Maybe she *had* lost her mind, Kathy mused. She wasn't making the slightest effort to remove herself from this stranger's arms. But the man's embrace was so soothing, so comfortable.

And she was intrigued. This man was the first bona fide rich Texan she'd ever seen in Dallas. She'd heard about them, but now she'd actually run into one. Literally.

"Are you hurt?"

His hands were skimming over her, looking for possible injuries. They were strong, competent hands, yet incredibly gentle. Distracted by his touch, she paused before answering him. "No."

He made a sudden sound of distress. "You're bleeding!"

"What?" Her fingers touched her forehead and came away stained with blood. "I must have hit myself on a sharp edge of the car door. I thought it was a wall."

"Robert double-parked the car." He shifted his position so that he could reach into his pocket, and beneath her, she felt a subtle movement of muscle and bone. Nice, she thought. Definitely nice. As he brought out an immaculately white handkerchief and lifted it to her forehead, she caught a glimpse of the monogram:—PG.

"The cut doesn't seem to be deep," he said.

She was sure it wasn't, but his care of her felt too good to allow her even to think of asking him to stop. Taking a deep, calming breath, she asked, "Who *are* you?"

"I'm Paul Garth."

The name meant nothing to her. But she supposed it didn't matter, since he was having the oddest effect on her. "I think it's very strange that you don't have a Texas accent," she said.

The expression in his blue eyes became so intent that all the gray seemed to disappear. "I don't think we can be too careful. I'm sure the hospital will want to X-ray. Head injuries can be tricky."

She heard only one word: *hospital*. It cleared her mind and brought her back to her senses as nothing else could have. Hospitals meant bills, and bills meant paying money she didn't have. She tried to scramble off his lap, but the hands she had thought so gentle suddenly tightened in a steely embrace.

"Don't move. You may be hurt worse than we know."

"Nonsense. I'm fine!" She wondered if the rather weak feeling in her limbs might have more to do with the man holding her than the accident.

An older man who was wearing a black uniform and cap bent to peer into the interior of the car. "Can I be of help, Mr. Garth?"

"Yes, Robert. We need to take"—he paused and looked at her inquiringly—"what is your name?"

"Kathy. Kathy Broderick."

"We need to take Kathy to the hospital right away."

There was that word again. "I tell you I'm all right!" This time she succeeded in escaping from his lap, and in her hurry to get out of the car, she almost ploughed into the very dignified Robert.

But at least she was standing on her own two feet and she was breathing in air that wasn't filled with the scent of Paul Garth. She felt much better, she assured herself, and was almost convinced. Then she saw her bent and mangled bicycle and had to fight off a queasy sensation. Blindly she reached out for the support of the dark, chocolate brown car.

The bicycle had been her only means of transportation! There was no bus that ran anywhere near her shop. What was she going to do?

Paul climbed out to stand beside her and nodded at the mangled bike. "Don't worry about the bicycle. Naturally, I'll see that it's replaced."

"Thank you, but that's not necessary." Although she felt weak, her voice was firm. To accept a brand-new bicycle in the place of her old, beat-up one wouldn't be right. "I should have been more careful. And the bike wasn't worth much. I bought it at a garage sale."

She didn't tell him about the amount of time she'd spent lovingly taking it apart and putting it back together again. She'd refinished the frame, sanded away any sign of rust, and painted it. She'd greased the bearings and oiled the wheels and chain. Although the bike didn't have any material worth, its value to her couldn't be measured.

She tore her gaze away from the bent and twisted frame and managed a smile. "Really," she added.

*She wasn't going to fall apart! She could handle this! She could!*

He moved closer to her, a concerned expression on his face. Ruefully she realized that his nearness still affected her, even though she was no longer in his arms. His brown hair gleamed with health and expert styling. His suit was of classic design. Made of a lightweight blue wool worsted and double-breasted, the suit's exquisite tailoring showed him to be a man of taste and sophistication. But she was sure the clothes weren't making the man. His tall, athletic body exuded an air of authority and command. And over and above all of that, she found him just plain sexy as hell. It didn't seem quite fair that she had to deal with him *and* the loss of her bike all in the same day.

He slipped his hands in the pockets of his pants, even as his brows drew together in a frown. "The value doesn't matter. The fact is, your bike was destroyed, and I'll see that it is replaced."

She supposed his impatience with her was warranted. Obviously, the man could buy her a top-of-the-line bicycle without making the slightest dent in his wallet. But a strong sense of honor had been bred into her bones, and she had to do what she thought was right.

Her brief sigh was Kathy's only visible sign of regret. "Look, this was all my fault. If I hadn't been looking for snow, I would have seen you."

Paul studied the slim, pale young woman in front of him, unsure what to make of her. She intrigued him, thought he couldn't really say why. She was one of the few people he had come across in recent years who didn't seem to want anything from him. And there was something in those beautiful green eyes of hers; a strong will and intelligence shone in them.

In the next moment, though, he realized the attraction was far more complicated than that. For he suddenly understood that this woman had caught him completely off guard. His reaction was far stronger than usual. They'd merely had a minor accident, and yet this woman evoked feelings of solicitude and protectiveness. Strangely he found himself wanting to stay close to her, wanting to watch over her. It was an utterly ridiculous notion.

Uneasy under his scrutiny, Kathy bent to pick up what was left of her bicycle.

"Robert," Paul said quietly,

The driver quickly took the pieces out of her hand. "Where would you like me to take this, miss?"

She might have argued that she could handle it, but she decided against it. She had no desire to wrestle with the dignified Robert. "If you could just prop it up over there by that door"—she pointed toward her shop—"I'd appreciate it."

Her encounter with this dream man was over now. It was time to face the real world where she couldn't even afford Scotch tape to help her make ends meet. Wasn't it ironic the way things worked? she asked herself. She couldn't afford a skate board, and yet she had run into the limousine of a man who could afford everything.

"I'm sorry I ran into your car." A bright smile was firmly fixed on her face when she turned back to Paul. "It's very nice, by the way. I don't believe I've ever seen a car quite so long. I hope I didn't do any damage to it. If I did, please send the bill to 'Kathy's Crafts and Decorations.' " She pointed toward the shop, then started to walk away.

"Wait." He reached into the inside pocket of his suit jacket and brought out a slim leather folder. Opening it, he retrieved a business card. "Take this. Both my office and home phone numbers are on it. If any latent injuries appear, call me at once. Promise?"

Without even glancing at the card, she stuffed it in the pocket of her jeans and turned.

Watching her walk away, Paul was left feeling as though there was unfinished business between them, something that had nothing to do with the accident.

What had she said? She'd been looking for snow?

Kathy Broderick bothered him. To begin with, she was too slender. She'd been light as a feather on his lap. With his arms around her, he had been able to feel the delicacy of her bones. The thought of how easily those bones could have been broken made his blood turn several degrees cooler. She should have someone to take care of her, he thought, then wondered if she did.

Her skin had been translucently clear and pale, except for an intriguing sprinkle of freckles across her nose. And her hair . . . it was a honey red, and she'd worn it in a ponytail. He couldn't remember the last time he'd seen anyone over the age of ten wear a ponytail. How long would her hair be, he wondered, if the honey red strands were allowed to spill down her back?

Robert appeared at his elbow. "Is there anything else you'd like me to attend to, sir?"

Kathy had disappeared into the shop, and he could no longer see her. He shook his head, both in answer to Robert and in an effort to clear his mind. "No. I'll be taking a quick tour of the village. I shouldn't be long."

"Very good, sir."

"Oh, and Robert? Move the car off the street so it isn't a danger to anyone."

"Yes, sir."

With his mind on business now, he set out to look over the newest acquisition of the Steele Corporation. The horseshoe-shaped village contained more than a dozen quaint, tidy shops. Nevertheless, their stucco facades were in need of patching and a good paint job. A number of the red Spanish roof tiles were missing. Grass grew between jagged cracks in the sidewalks. A large, round fountain stood in the center of the village, leaves and grass filling it instead of water. According to his report, the fountain hadn't worked in years. Well, all of that was about to change. Bluebonnet Village was going to be brought into the mainstream of the Dallas business community—very soon.

Kathy settled onto the stool behind the counter and waited for the sights and smells of her shop to soothe her.

There was an entire wall of shelves filled with brightly colored yarn. Another wall held festive spools of ribbons. And there were three armoires that she'd spent weeks refinishing. One held bouquets of dried flowers and large bowls of potpourri. Another held folded afghans, shawls, and quilts, which she sold on consignment for some of her customers. The third held an assortment of stuffed animals.

Kathy had carefully selected and arranged all of it, from the needlework materials to the folk art and tole paints, craft books, rug hooking-supplies, and so much more. She loved everything about her shop. But today the warm, happy feeling the shop usually gave her seemed to elude her. Now, more than ever before, she realized that this shop was the culmination of a lifelong dream. But dreams were expensive, and she had a stack of bills in front of her to prove it.

Each month she held her breath, wondering whether this would be the month she wouldn't be able to pay all her bills. And now she didn't have transportation. She sighed. Well, she would just have to leave her apartment an hour or so earlier and walk to the store. Well, big deal, she decided.

With her resolve and determination intact, she reached for the letter on top of the stack of bills. The return address showed that it was from a real estate management firm. Curious, Kathy slit open the envelope.

A minute later, the letter slipped from her lifeless fingers. She couldn't believe it! The village had been sold—and the new owners were raising her rent by five hundred dollars! She dropped her head in her hands. It might as well have been five thousand dollars. At the moment, she didn't see how she could afford even five extra dollars! She'd already cut expenditures to the bone. What on earth was she going to do?

Tears gathered in her eyes, but determinedly she lifted her head. This was just another problem to solve, that was all. On an average day she probably solved a hundred problems. She would handle this predicament, just as she would cope with the dilemma of no transportation, no food, and no snow in the month of December. And she wouldn't cry! She *never* cried!

As her empty stomach growled, her gaze lighted on the small bowl of M & M's chocolate candies that she kept for the children. At least she'd found one solution!

It wasn't a conscious decision that made Paul head toward Kathy's Crafts and Decorations when he completed his walking tour of the village. Rather it was an automatic reflex that he didn't question. As he stepped onto the sidewalk in front of the shop, a hail of small, multicolored objects went flying past the large storefront window.

He rushed through the door. "What's wrong? What's happened?"

Shocked by his sudden presence, Kathy quickly swatted at her cheeks, attempting to wipe away the traces of her tears. "Nothing."

"Then what was that shower of things I just saw sailing by the window?"

"The contents of a bowl of M and M's that had no green ones in it." She wiped at her face again, wishing the tears would stop falling. "See, I have two brothers and two sisters. When we were little, my mother would buy one bag of M and M's and divide it between us."

Her tears hadn't escaped his attention. "Kathy, what's wrong?"

"I'm trying to tell you," she snapped a little indignantly. "You can imagine, can't you, that with five children and very little money for treats, Mother had to divide the candy. But it worked out. We were each assigned a color. Mark got the tans, Anna, the browns, Margaret, the oranges, and Peter, the yellows. Mother always took the reds, except in the seventies, of course, when they were pulled because Red Dye No. Two was suspected of causing cancer in laboratory animals." She sniffed. "I got the green M and M's. They've always been my favorite."

Paul decided that further questioning wouldn't help. "I was right. You were hurt far worse than we suspected."

"No, no, I'm fine." She waved her hand in the vague direction of the candy scattered over the floor. "It's just that I always try to keep a bowl of candy for my customers' children. I don't usually eat it, but this morning I decided to nibble on a couple of pieces. But when I found out all the green ones were gone, it was the final straw. You understand?" She sniffed one last time, grateful that at least the tears seemed to have stopped.

But when he lifted his hand to gently touch the cut on her forehead, her senses went spinning. How could she keep herself from flying apart around this unsettling man?

"The cut hasn't swelled, but I definitely want to take you to the hospital."

"Mr. Garth—"

"Paul," he corrected in a soft tone that sent a shimmering warmth spreading through her, banishing all rational thought from her mind.

"Paul, you don't understand. I couldn't afford to go to a hospital even if I needed to—which I don't. Besides, I don't like hospitals. They smell terrible. And inside, they're always white!"

"There's no need to worry about the cost of medical treatment. I intend to take care of any bills," he insisted.

"I'm sure you do, but I can't allow that." With the greatest of efforts, she forced a smile onto her face, noticing that an ache was forming at the base of her skull.

He studied her for a moment. He'd never met anyone so determined to refuse his help. And, ironically, the desire to help her had been growing in him since she'd landed in his lap. It was a desire he couldn't ignore, a vague feeling he couldn't as yet put his finger on.

Paul read the lettering on the black sweatshirt she was wearing. *John, Paul, George, and Ringo.* He smiled. "Are you always this stubborn?"

"Always. I'm from New England." She glanced out the window. "They already have snow up there."

"No doubt. Look, isn't there anything you'll let me do for you?"

"You've been very kind, but no. Now if you'll excuse me, I need to straighten up before the customers start arriving." She turned away, saying a short, silent prayer that customers actually *would* arrive.

The muscles in Paul's jaw tightened, a small indication of his frustration. She wanted him to leave, and he had no logical reason to stay. But as he walked out the door, he was plagued by a hollow sense of dissatisfaction.

It had been a really rotten Monday, Kathy concluded, flipping the OPEN sign to CLOSED. Every one of her fellow shopkeepers in the village had received a letter similar to hers. And the news had been particularly devastating to Mrs. Armbruster, the sweet, elderly Texas belle whose tearoom occupied the space next to her craft shop.

Kathy had an agreement with the older woman; Kathy supplied seasonal centerpieces for the cafe's tables, and in return, Mrs. Armbruster provided a free lunch at two o'clock every afternoon, after the tearoom had closed. However, today Mrs. Armbruster had been so upset over the rent increase, she had closed the tearoom and gone home. Kathy had missed the one meal she usually counted on.

To make matters worse, her prayer for customers hadn't been answered. Only Mrs. Jacobson and Mrs. Kendricks had come in. But as was the case with most of her regular customers, the two ladies were retired and lived on a fixed income. They had to keep their purchases small and frugal. At times, Kathy actually had to stop herself from giving the sweet ladies a generous discount.

Kathy put a hand to her pounding head and glanced around, trying to remember what else needed to be done before she left. Worry, added to a day without eating, had sharpened her headache into a full-scale migraine, and she had no idea how she was going to manage to walk the four miles to her tiny apartment.

The sight of the long, brown limousine pulling up in front of the store didn't help matters. Despite her concern over finances and the increasing pain of her headache, Paul Garth hadn't been out of her thoughts all day long.

At one point during the day, she'd discovered herself trying to pick out blue and gray ribbons that matched the color of his eyes. Another time, she found herself hugging a calico teddy bear to her breast, remembering how Paul's strong arms had felt around her. Now he was here, and even though her head was pounding, she felt excitement twist and turn its way through her at the prospect of seeing him again.

Truly confident people were surrounded by a certain aura, and Paul Garth was no exception, Kathy decided, as he entered her shop a minute later. She was sure that it was only the second time he'd ever been inside a craft store—this morning being the first—yet he seemed completely at ease.

"Are you ready to leave?" he asked.

She didn't dare nod her head. "I'm closing up, but if there's something you need, I'd be glad to stay open a few more minutes."

His smile was a sweeping wave of charm. "I've come to take you home."

"That's not necessary," she said automatically.

His eyes narrowed. If he had thought her pale this morning, she was positively colorless now. There had never been any doubt in his mind that he would come back this evening. Now he wished he'd returned sooner. "Is someone else picking you up?"

"No."

"You've called a cab?"

"No."

"Oh, then you must have bought another bike."

"No."

"Then you need a ride home, don't you?"

She licked her lips. It wasn't fair. She'd had a hard time resisting this magnetic man earlier in the day. Now that she was hurting so badly that she could barely see, she had no defense against him.

With a sigh of surrender, she reached for her keys.

# Two

"I live in the back, above the garage," she told Paul as his driver pulled the big car into the driveway of the address she had given. Robert heard her and proceeded around to the back of the house situated in an old, quiet neighborhood.

Tall trees clustered around the small garage apartment. At the sound of the approaching car, a squirrel skittered across a branch and disappeared among a festival of red-gold leaves that were still stubbornly keeping their hold on life.

Paul leaned forward and peered through the tinted window. "Do you live here alone?"

"Yes. I like it a lot. It's the first time I've ever had a place of my own. With so many brothers and sisters, I never had the luxury of my own room." Kathy knew she was babbling, but she needed to distract Paul—and herself—from the pain that was blossoming in her head. "I have a great deal of privacy here, since the couple who own the house travel a lot."

He glanced at the two-story red brick house. "Are they home now?"

His words seemed to come from a distance. With great effort, she responded, "No. They're spending the winter in Florida. It seems to me, though, that they could have just as easily stayed here. It's certainly not at all cold." As Robert drew the long car to a halt, she gazed at the stairs that led to her second-story apartment. *If I can make it up those stairs, I'll be all right.* "The only reason for them to go to Florida is so they can see the ocean. You have to admit, Dallas doesn't have an ocean."

"No, we've never had one of those, although I'd be willing to bet that the city planners have looked into the possibility of acquiring one."

She glanced back at him, her green eyes almost glazed over with pain. "What?"

The smile he gave her was gentle. "You don't even know what you're saying, do you? What's the matter, Kathy? Tell me. I know you're not well."

She licked her upper lip. "I just have a headache. Nothing serious."

He stiffled a curse. It was more than just a headache, and he knew it. "Do you have anything to take for it?"

"No. I rarely have headaches.'

"And certainly never one this bad?'

"Right."

His mouth tensed.

Kathy closed her eyes. Drat, but her honesty slipped out at the most inopportune times! She was going to have to be more careful!

"Robert, take us to the—"

"Wait! If you say the word hospital one more time, I'm going to scream. And I never, ever scream!"

"Kathy, I only want to help you."

She thrust out a hand and encountered his hard arm. Without thinking, she let her fingers wrap around it. Somehow his strength made her feel steadier. "You've got to understand. This headache has nothing to do with the accident. It's just a plain, run-of-the-mill, screechingly painful headache." The exertion of pronouncing each word drained her, but she had to make him believe that she was okay. "And what's more, its cause isn't very mysterious. I forgot to eat today, that's all."

"Are you sure?"

Her natural reticence against burdening someone else with her problems made her omit the letter from the realtor that had worried her all day. "I'm sure. Things were so busy in the shop today, I didn't have time for lunch." For a moment, she wrestled with the guilt of telling him a lie, but the pain in her head made her conscience fade.

"Okay, then let's go upstairs and get some food into you. If that doesn't make you feel better—"

She panicked, knowing that she couldn't let him see the barren state of her kitchen. "There's no need for you to come up with me. You must be terribly busy and all. Riding around in this car must take up a lot of your time. And the responsibility of it—I can't even imagine."

"Kathy, stop arguing and save your breath! From the looks of you, I'll be surprised if you can make it up those stairs. But if you can't, don't worry, because I certainly won't mind carrying you."

The thought momentarily took Kathy's mind off her pain.

Robert opened the car door. Paul climbed out, then extended his hand for her. Getting out of the car made the throbbing ache in Kathy's head worsen. In the end, Paul did have to carry her up the stairs.

Kathy's apartment consisted of only two rooms—the bedroom and the living room-kitchen area. She had lovingly furnished it with a few pieces salvaged from garage sales and Goodwill Industries. The dark red upholstered couch and chair had seen better days in the forties, but they were supremely comfortable. A floor lamp provided excellent light, despite the fact that its shade was missing half its fringe. And the wooden coffee table had a long, thin crack down its center. In one corner, an old card table held an assortment of silk poinsettias, greenery, and ribbon, which she'd gathered to make Christmas displays for the store.

She kept her little apartment scrupulously neat, and it had never occurred to her to be ashamed of it. Fleetingly, though, she wished that the occasion of having a guest for the first time could have been different. Then she chastised herself. Paul Garth wasn't a guest. He was simply a very nice man who felt responsible for her.

Without asking, he took her straight into the

bedroom and placed her carefully on the bed. "Now, I want you to undress and get into bed, while I see about making you something to eat."

Turning her aching head into the pillow, she mumbled, "If I sleep, I'll be all right. Why don't you go on home . . . unless, of course, you sleep in the car. I would understand if you did . . . since I'm sure it cost you more than the average home."

As Paul looked down at her, he saw her wince. Her pain completely unnerved him. He felt desperate, driven to erase it completely. Unable to stand by helplessly and watch her suffer, he strode out of the small bedroom and into the kitchen, determined to do something to help her.

Minutes later, he stood by the sink, baffled. His search of the cabinets had produced only one small can of tuna and two cans of pork and beans. And the refrigerator was almost as bare as the shelves. Holding the refrigerator door open, he counted four items: a box of oatmeal, a nearly empty quart of skim milk, a jar of peanut butter, and a bread bag that had no bread in it.

He was surprised that Kathy had so little food in her kitchen. He snatched the empty bread bag and practically slammed the door shut. He filled the bag with ice cubes from a tray in the freezer, grabbed up a clean dishtowel, then returned to Kathy's side.

"You haven't changed clothes yet," he murmured, sitting down beside her.

"I decided not to," she whispered. "My head doesn't hurt as much if I don't move."

She was lying on her side, with half of her face pressed into the pillow. Angel-fine wisps of hair curled over her forehead. He reached out to stroke them off her brow. "Poor baby."

This morning she had fallen into his lap like some sort of gift, and for the first time since his wife's death, Paul had had an emotional reaction to a woman. Kathy didn't know it yet, but he was going to be around for a while. She needed someone to take care of her, and he needed someone to make him *feel* again.

He wrapped the plastic bag in the dishtowel, then gently placed it on her head. "This should make you feel better. And this." He slipped off the rubber band holding her ponytail, and her red hair spilled free. "I've been wanting to do that ever since I met you." He combed her hair out with his fingers, then began to massage her scalp.

"Mmmm, that's wonderful! You have strong hands. Do you play the piano?"

He laughed softly. "No."

"That's too bad. I love music."

"What kind?"

"All kinds. Except Muzak."

She turned her head slightly so that he could reach another spot. Beneath the hard pressure of his fingers, she could almost feel the tight pain fading away. She definitely had a tension headache. Kathy usually didn't let things get to her. But then again, the prospect of losing her shop certainly surpassed the minor impact of everyday annoyances.

"What else do you love?" he asked her.

"I love my shop," she answered softly and without hesitation.

"Tell me about it."

"Will you keep up the massage?"

He grinned. He'd continue the massage until his fingers fell off, if it would make her feel better. "As long as you like."

She gave a contented sigh. "I think it's helping. And about the shop . . . let's see . . ." She shut her eyes and let her mind drift away from the ache in her head. "Last year, in December, actually, I received my degree in liberal arts. It took me forever. I had to work so much, along with attending school. I'm twenty-six, pretty old to be in school. But I finally graduated . . . That *really* feels good! Anyway, I couldn't decide what I wanted to do, but I'd had a lot of business courses, so I sent out my résumé. I was hired by a company here in Dallas, and I moved down. Unfortunately the firm suddenly had to cut back its staff, and I was one of the first to get the pink slip. I tried to get another job, but with no experience . . . and I guess it's obvious I'm not exactly the button-down type, although I did try. But there were always plenty of other applicants ahead of me who looked great in tailored suits. I don't even own one."

Without stopping his massage, Paul shifted the ice bag to another place on her head. Her red hair was flowing over his hand, wrist, and arm. When he had first seen her that morning, he had somehow known her hair would be like this, luxuriant, glistening and silky.

"I discovered Bluebonnet Village one afternoon

while I was riding my bicycle around town, and I fell in love with it. It was like a place that time had passed by. One of the stores was for lease. Since I'd always been interested in crafts, I decided to draw on the business knowledge I'd picked up in college and start my own shop. It sounded so easy at the time."

"What did you do about financing?" he asked, then wondered at the anxious lines that formed on her forehead.

"I borrowed the money from a friend, and agreed to pay her back at current market price." Toni Sinclair had been wonderful, Kathy remembered, and just as excited about the shop as she had been. By lending her the money, Toni had exhibited a faith in her that meant the world to Kathy. The fact that Toni could easily afford the loan changed nothing. No matter what, Kathy was determined to make Toni's investment pay off.

"Relax," he murmured, feeling her scalp tighten beneath his fingers. "Whatever it is that's worrying you can't be that bad."

So she hadn't entirely fooled him. Paul knew something was bothering her, and he was right. But he was wrong about one thing: today's events were even worse than he could imagine.

Kathy was the first person in her family to attempt an independent business. For years her older sister had been a housekeeper for Linc Sinclair, Toni's husband. Kathy had another brother still in college. She had thought that once the shop was established, she could help him. Her youngest brother and sister were still at home.

She'd wanted to help them too. She'd had such grand plans, and her family was so proud of her. But how could she explain that to a man who wore his success as casually as other men wore after-shave?

Paul picked up the ice bag. "I need to get more ice for this." He hesitated. "Do you think you could eat something? I'll call Robert and send him out for some dinner."

"Your car may have a phone, but my apartment doesn't." She was thinking more clearly now, and she forestalled any questions by adding, "The phone at the shop is all I need."

Paul had to bite his tongue to prevent an exclamation. As time passed, he was getting a clear picture of Kathy's situation, and he didn't like what he was seeing one bit. "Then I'll go downstairs and give him our order. There's a Chinese place not far from here."

She rolled over on her back and found that the pain had eased. "That's not necessary. I can make myself something later."

"There's not much in the way of food in your kitchen," he said casually. 'You must eat out a lot. By the way, why do you keep oatmeal in your refrigerator?"

"Because two mice share this apartment with me, and they'll get in the oatmeal if I leave the box in the cupboard."

"Why not kill them?"

"Why should I? They're trying to get along in this world as best they can, just like everyone else is. What's so bad about that? But I can't let them get in the box. If they ate the oatmeal raw, their little tummies would swell up."

She sounded genuinely sad about the fact, he thought, amused. Any other woman wouldn't rest until an exterminator had put an end to the mice. But she was concerned for them. Unable to resist, he reached out and stroked her forehead, careful not to touch the wounded area. "So what do you want to eat?"

"I told you—"

"Kathy—" He leaned over her and positioned his hands on either side of her. Her eyes had lost that glazed look, he noted, relieved. "I haven't known you very long, but already I've learned that you're too damned stubborn and independent!"

She swallowed hard. "Too damned stubborn and independent for what?"

"For your own good—and my piece of mind. You wouldn't let me get you medical help when I thought you needed it, but you're not going to stop me from sending Robert out for some food. So, shall I choose something or would you like to?

Now that her headache had quieted, food did sound good. And if she agreed, she'd get to spend some more time with Paul before he disappeared from her life. "Okay. You choose."

Sitting across from Kathy at the small dinette table, Paul watched her take the last spoonful of wonton soup. "Did you like it?"

"Very much." The flavorful and nourishing chicken broth of the soup's base had really hit the spot, and she was feeling a hundred percent better.

"I probably don't dine out as much as you do, but I've always found the food at this particular restaurant very good."

Kathy turned her attention to the rice, not trusting herself to comment. Because her refrigerator and cupboards were bare, Paul thought that she ate out. If he only knew!

"So how's your headache?"

"Almost gone," she said. "The scalp massage and ice and the food have really helped. I'm just sorry I've put you to so much trouble."

"When you know me better, you'll realize I don't do anything I don't want to do."

Kathy swallowed hard. No man had ever been able to speed up the beating of her heart as this man could, and her reaction scared her. *Men like Paul just don't fall for girls like you.* She hadn't really thought about it before now, but the reason had to have something to do with the laws of nature, two completely different types of people should never be together. Soon Paul would exit from her life. If she started him on his way now, before too much hurt and anxiety were involved, she would be much better off.

She laid her fork down and rested her forearms on the table. "Look, I know that you feel some sort of responsibility for me. But there's really no need. I'm fine now."

He grinned and Kathy shifted uncomfortably. It was as if he could see right through her.

"I did feel responsible—at first. But if that had

been all I felt, I guarantee you, my staff of lawyers would have handled the matter."

In the dim light of her little kitchen, she couldn't help but notice how amazingly blue his eyes were. With his jacket off and his shirtsleeves rolled up, he looked relaxed and comfortable. His shirt was white with a tiny blue stripe running through the fine oxford cloth. He had pushed his chair away from the table and was lazing back in it with the ankle of one leg placed over the other leg. He appeared very much at home. Apparently she just wasn't getting through to him!

"Paul,"—the flat of her hand smacked the Formica of the table—"We live in two different worlds. You ride in a limousine, I ride a bicycle! Or at least I did!"

He smiled, ignoring her objection. "I'm a widower, Kathy. My wife, Sarah, died five years ago."

"Paul, I'm so sorry!"

"Listen to me, Kathy. I'm not telling you this to gain your sympathy. For five years, my wife's friends have, with all the best intentions, been throwing me together with various companions. I won't deny that I've spent time with quite a few women, but none of them have come close to completely capturing my attention. You have."

She laughed nervously. "Well, of course. I crashed into your car."

"I should give Robert a raise for double-parking in that particular spot."

She leaped to her feet, took a few steps, then stopped, not quite sure where she was going. And anyway, how could she escape from him in a two-room apartment? And did she really want to?

She felt foolish trying to talk Paul out of being attracted to her. But for reasons of honor, the laws of nature, and avoiding any further worry and pain, she felt driven to keep trying.

"And then, after crashing into you, I threw the M and M's across the shop and burst into tears. The third time you saw me, I had a blinding headache and you had to take care of me." She linked her fingers together and stared down at them. "You've only seen me at my worst, you know."

He rose and went to her, curling his hands around her arms. "If that's the case, I'm not sure my heart would take seeing you at your best, because, lady, you knock my socks off."

"But why?" she asked, bewildered and breathless.

He flicked her cheek with his finger. "Maybe because I've never known a woman who eats only green M and M's and seems so preoccupied by the weather."

His hand slipped beneath the heavy fall of her hair to the back of her neck, and his mouth pressed a gentle good-night kiss to her lips. The problem was, the kiss was so shatteringly sensitive, she was left feeling as fragile as a piece of crystal.

Kathy was always awake by dawn's first light, and the next morning was no exception. The habit of waking early irritated her almost as much as the we-won't-have-any-snow-this-year attitude that Dallas seemed to cling to so stubbornly, but she wasn't able to do much about either.

She threw back the covers and sat up, recalling how her night's sleep had been filled with dreams of Paul. Dreaming of him seemed entirely appropriate, since to her he *was* a dream man. He was kind and good-looking, and she could easily recall the warmth she'd felt at his kiss. She supposed she could add considerate to his list of sterling qualities, because right after the kiss, he'd told her to get some rest, then quietly slipped out the door.

She wasn't sure whether or not she would see him again. It might be for the best if she didn't. As Hemingway wrote in "The Snows of Kilimanjaro," "The very rich are different from you and me." She came from a working-class family. Her friendship with Toni and Linc Sinclair had been a breakthrough of sorts. The relationship had shown her that the privileged and the talented could have just as many problems as those with fewer worldly goods. But Toni and Linc had been two of a kind. She and Paul weren't.

An accident had brought him into her life. But a man who wore custom-tailored suits and rode in a big, chocolate brown car could only be a temporary visitor in Kathy's life.

The voice of the weatherman on the radio intruded into her thoughts. "It's going to be another beautiful day in Dallas, Texas! The temperature today is going to climb all the way up to seventy-four degrees, and the wind is going to be out of the south. Aren't we lucky!"

Kathy stuck her tongue out at the radio and clicked it off. "I'm going to quit listening to you," she muttered. There had to be other weathermen in town who could get some cold, Christmas weather into the area!

After a trip to the bathroom, she took a brush to her hair. As she did, a random memory from the night before entered her mind, a vague impression of Paul slipping the rubber band from her ponytail, saying that he'd been wanting to do that. And she definitely remembered the way his fingers had combed through her hair and moved over her scalp. It had been an intimate act, and he'd been excessively gentle and caring. She tossed the hairbrush down, and, on impulse, decided to leave her hair loose so that it rippled freely around her shoulders and down her back, like a waterfall of red-gold sunshine.

She pulled on a pair of jeans, and after some thought, passed by her assortment of sweatshirts in favor of an off-white blouse and a rust pullover. She planned on visiting the new realtor today and wanted to look as nice as possible.

In the kitchen, a peek into her refrigerator was discouraging. She supposed she could make herself more oatmeal, but she usually saved that for a dinner meal. She could have a glass of milk, but then she wouldn't have any milk for the oatmeal tonight, and the thought of a spoonful of peanut butter turned her stomach.

She shut the refrigerator with a grimace. "Oh, well." She didn't have time, anyway. Without her bike, she had a four-mile walk ahead of her. "Bye, mice," she called as she went out the door.

As she walked out onto the small landing, she

saw the long, gleaming, brown limousine parked in the driveway. Paul was leaning against the car, reading the paper. When he heard the door, he looked up and a smile spread across his face. "Good morning! How are you feeling?"

"Fine. My headache's completely gone." She paused and rested her hand on the railing. "What are you doing here?"

He handed the paper to Robert, who had appeared from out of the depths of the car. "Several things, but mainly waiting for you."

She descended the stairs and walked across the drive to him, unable to believe that this amazing man had once again shown up in her life. And just when she'd almost convinced herself that it would be better if she never saw him again! Now what? She wondered, nodding to Robert. "Morning."

With great formality, he tipped his cap to her. "Good morning, miss."

Without taking his gaze from her, Paul said, "I'll get the door, Robert."

"Very good, sir." The chauffeur walked around the car and disappeared into the front seat.

Nervous and hesitant, she flipped her hair behind her shoulder. "It's very early."

"I wanted to get here in time to take you to work."

"That wasn't necessary. I was going to, uh . . ."

"Walk?" Paul supplied helpfully.

"There's nothing wrong with walking. It's excellent exercise for the heart."

"So is this."

He drew her into his arms, and the kiss he gave her was as soft as the morning, without force, without demand. Yet inside Kathy desire stirred. It seemed entirely natural to lean against him, to let him support her weight, so that she could concentrate on the kiss.

His fingers burrowed through her hair and tightened. "I like your hair loose," he murmured, and then he was kissing her again.

Her arms crept around his neck, and he pulled her closer into him. The pressure of her breasts against his chest was an aching pleasure.

Daringly she darted her tongue into his mouth and discovered that he tasted like everything she'd ever been hungry for. Delicious. With a little more of this, she could become addicted. And if that happened, it would be very hard to ever get enough to feel satisfied. Even now . . .

She sighed as sweetness and heat fused. When it came to matters of the heart, Kathy was a novice. She'd had a variety of boyfriends over the years, but her heart had never been involved. Now, though, all sorts of new emotions and unknown passions were winding through her, like pretty ribbons looping and lacing around her heart. It was heady . . . and frightening.

"Paul." His name came from her, a soft entreaty that was filled with both desire and uncertainty.

Paul drew in a ragged breath. He didn't want to end the kiss, but he knew if he didn't stop now, he would rapidly arrive at the point of no return. This wasn't the right place or time. She wasn't ready. And perhaps he was too ready.

He took a step back from her, and his gaze went to the moist, just-kissed fullness of her lips, then to her eyes. They were like emeralds, sparkling in the sunlight. He, who was always on top of every situation, found that his control was extremely tenuous.

He grazed his thumb over her bottom lip. "Are you hungry?"

Pride rushed forward. "No. I, uh, already ate."

He reached around behind him and opened the door. "That's too bad, because I've arranged breakfast for us. Maybe you can eat a little something."

She climbed into the back of the car and settled into the seat with surprise. In front of her, a linen-covered table had been set up at knee height. Two elegant place settings had been arranged, along with silver dome-covered dishes. The enticing aroma of coffee and bacon filled the big car.

Paul got in beside her and shut the door. "Robert, just drive around for a while, will you?"

"Yes, sir."

"What is all this?" She was having a hard time keeping her mouth from watering.

"I told you, breakfast. Here." He spooned some scrambled eggs onto her plate and added three pieces of bacon. "You might want to take a bite or two."

She pressed her hand over her empty stomach. "It looks like you went to a lot of trouble. I suppose it'd be a shame not to taste it at least."

"I was hoping you'd say that. Orange juice?"

"Maybe just half a glass."

He nodded. "Biscuits and honey?"

"Perhaps just one."

"Good."

The food was melting in her mouth. She'd never tasted anything so good in all her life, but she forced herself to eat with moderation. She couldn't let him see how desperately hungry she was. The last thing she wanted from him was pity.

Paul sipped his coffee and watched her.

With great effort she put down her fork, deciding to wait a minute or two before her next bite. "Why aren't you eating?"

Dutifully, he filled his plate. "Have you tried the bacon yet?"

She looked at the crisp brown strips on her plate with longing. "No."

"You must try it. Here, have a bite of mine." He thrust a piece of bacon into her mouth. "Good?"

She nodded, chewing. "Mmmm."

"And how about this honey?" He shoved a substantial portion of a honey-laden biscuit into her mouth. "It's made from bees raised right here in Texas."

"Mmmm."

As the long car rolled through the streets of Dallas, the tinted windows kept out the gazes of curious passersby. Paul, food, and luxury, Kathy thought. It was a fantasy that she wished she could just relax and enjoy. But reality was waiting for her at the shop in the form of the troubling letter, and she had to do something about it.

Paul had unknowingly solved one of her more immediate problems of the day: hunger. Now it was up to her to solve the other problem: the sizable rent increase. Surely the real estate firm would be reasonable when she explained the situation to them.

There was just one other little thing that was bothering her. She couldn't figure out how to get to the realtor's office.

When she bit down on a ripe, juicy strawberry that had somehow found its way into her mouth, she held up her hand in protest. "That's enough! Remember, I told you, I've already eaten."

"That's right. I must have forgotten." He grinned and leaned toward her. "You've got honey and strawberry juice all over your chin." Before she could reach for her napkin, his moist lips began the cleaning-up chore. "Lord, you taste good," he whispered.

Kathy's breath lodged in her chest so that she was unable to either inhale or exhale. She couldn't talk, either. Warmth was unfolding in her stomach and spreading a heated feeling all through her. She finally managed to say, "That's not me. You're tasting the strawberries and honey."

"Let's see." He trailed light kisses up her face until he reached the freckles that graced her nose and upper cheeks. Then, one by one, he tasted and kissed them. "You're wrong," he murmured a few minutes later. "You're sweet here, too. I bet you're sweet all over."

She couldn't be anything but honest. "If you don't stop, I'm going to melt all over this very expensive leather upholstery."

He gave a low laugh. "I wouldn't mind at all. In fact, in the very near future, I plan to devote a great deal of time to finding out the exact point at which you'll melt. And I will find out." He threw a brief glance out the window. "But since we're at your shop . . ."

The back of her head was resting against the seat. Her voice was dreamy. "We're where?"

"In front of your shop."

Her head snapped up. "Oh!"

Critically, he eyed her still half-full plate. "Did you get enough to eat?"

"Oh, plenty. I'm stuffed." In fact, she could have easily eaten what was left on her plate and his, too, but she couldn't bring herself to tell him.

"Good, then let's get out. I've got something for you."

He was already out the door before she could collect her senses. She scrambled after him and followed him to the back of the car. Robert was there, raising the trunk lid.

Paul reached down into the cavernous opening, pulled out an obviously expensive, sleek, green, ten-speed bicycle, and set it on the ground in front of her. "This is to replace the one that got attacked by my car yesterday."

"What attacked what is debatable," she murmured, unable to tear her gaze from the bike. It was the most beautiful thing she'd ever seen, and something she desperately needed. She folded her hands together to keep from reaching out and grabbing the bicycle. "I—I can't accept it!"

"You're going to."

She looked up at him. Every once in a while she caught a glimpse of a man other than the nice, gentle Paul she was coming to know. Just then, his voice had been hard with authority. "I already told you. The accident was my fault."

"You don't have a car, do you?"

Her eyes widened in surprise. "No, of course not. I can't even drive. And it seems that everyone in Texas over the age of fifteen can. It makes me feel quite backward, but I didn't need to drive in Connecticut or New York. We had trains and buses and subways. And, anyway, driving is dangerous."

He laughed at that. "Do you need this bicycle, or don't you?"

She needed it so badly, she couldn't lie. "I need it."

"Then you're going to accept it."

Her mind raced, dredging up then discarding possibilities. She could walk the four miles to and from the shop every day, an eight-mile round trip. She could even manage to do her shopping without a bike. But the real estate company was located a considerable distance away, and it would be impossible for her to get there on foot. She didn't feel good about accepting the bike, but her back was up against a wall.

"All right. I'll accept it. And thank you."

"Good. Now about that other matter?"

She looked up, confused. "What other matter?"

He smiled. "Finding the point at which you will melt. Remember?"

Oh, yes. She definitely remembered. She was on the verge of melting with Paul's slightest touch.

"Have dinner with me," he persisted.

No man had ever made her want him so quickly. No man had ever insinuated himself into her life so fast. She could summon up all sorts of reasons to resist Paul, but why should she bother? Yesterday had been a definite low point in her life. Today was a new day. She was strong. She could handle Paul *and* her problems. At least she desperately wanted to believe that she could.

"Please, Kathy."

Feeling as though her common sense had just taken wing, like dandelion puffs flying away on the wind, she murmured, "All right."

Tenderly, he cupped her face in his hands. "Robert will pick you up after work and drive you home. I'll be by about seven-thirty."

"I can't wait," she admitted.

# Three

As it turned out, Kathy wasn't able to make it to the real estate company after all. She estimated the round trip on the bicycle, together with the meeting itself, would take at least three hours, and every time she started out the door, a customer came in. She needed the money so badly, she couldn't bring herself to close the shop. Unfortunately, only a few people actually made purchases.

In the late afternoon Kathy realized another very important reason why she shouldn't have accepted Paul's dinner invitation. She was sure that Paul planned to take her to one of Dallas's best restaurants. A man like Paul appreciated fine cuisine.

The problem was that, unlike millions of other American women, when Kathy said she didn't have a thing to wear, she *really* meant it. For two minutes, she allowed herself the luxury of panicking, then she calmed down and set about solving this, the newest of her problems.

There was a "gently used clothing" store in Bluebonnet Village. Kathy reluctantly closed her shop for fifteen minutes and hurried down the street.

The owner of the shop, a lovely middle-aged woman named Judith Beldon, met her at the door. "Kathy, how nice! We don't get to see enough of each other."

"That's true, we don't. But I'm afraid this isn't a social visit. I need your help."

"What can I do for you?" She waved her hand around the store to show that there were no customers. "As you can see, I'm not busy."

"I've got the same problem down at—" The sound of a dog barking in the back room interrupted Kathy. "Why do you have Lancelot back there? If someone comes to rob you, he won't be much help."

"Oh, I'll let him out in a minute. I just put him back there while I was sweeping up. He's always underfoot."

"Well, you did want him for protection, you know."

Judith laughed. "With the way business is these days, I'm not sure we have to worry about being robbed."

Kathy groaned. "I know. Well, at any rate, I'm going out this evening, and I've got nothing to wear."

"You've got a date! How exciting!"

"Don't say that. I'm trying to be calm about the whole thing."

"I've seen a limousine in front of your store

several times now. Does this date have anything to do with the car?"

Kathy laughed. "I have to admit, I first became involved with the car, but tonight I'm going out with its owner."

Judith's eyes widened. She was impressed. "That *is* exciting."

Kathy nodded. Just thinking about the evening ahead made her palms sweat. "Back to the reason why I'm here. Do you have something perfectly dazzling for me to wear? Something that will cost practically nothing?"

Judith frowned worriedly. "I don't think I have anything that matches that description. The problem is, no one has brought in anything stylish in so long, I'm about ready to give up." She snapped her fingers suddenly. "I just remembered something. A lady brought in a beautiful silk skirt the other day. She bought it for her teenage daughter, then decided it was too sophisticated for the girl. Just a minute."

Judith disappeared into her back room, then emerged holding a short, narrow, gold silk skirt in one hand and a pair of gold high-heeled shoes in the other. "Good news! I found shoes to match. That is, if you can wear size six shoes."

"I can. But Judith, the skirt! I've never worn anything that sultry before. Or sexy!"

"It'll look great on you, trust me. I just hope you have a blouse that will go with it, because I don't have a thing."

Kathy's heart sank. "I don't have a decent blouse to my name."

"What about a little tank top? Silk?"

"Nope."

"Okay. How about a knockout sweater? Maybe something in cream? Cashmere would be great."

"No."

Judith groaned. "Well . . . how about one of those big fifty-inch scarves?"

"No . . . yes! I do! My friend Toni gave me one. It's a paisley print in green, teal, and rust, and it has a beautiful gold thread running through it."

"That's great! I'll tell you what to do with it."

"Wait a minute." Reluctantly Kathy held up a hand to put a halt to Judith's mounting enthusiasm. "You haven't mentioned the price of the skirt and the shoes. I wasn't joking when I said it needs to cost practically nothing."

"I tell you what, I'll let you wear the skirt and shoes tonight as sort of a professional courtesy. Just return them tomorrow."

"Are you sure?"

"Absolutely. And maybe I'll come down to your shop in a day or two and buy some greenery and stuff for a centerpiece, and you can put it together for me."

Kathy grabbed Judith's hand and shook it. "Deal. Now, tell me what in the world I do with the scarf."

Kathy didn't have to look at the clock to know that it was nearly seven-thirty. She could tell the time by counting the number of butterflies in her stomach. She cast another look at herself in the mirror, still not sure what to make of the image that greeted her.

Following Judith's instructions to the letter, she'd taken the scarf and tied a knot in the middle of it on the underside. She had then tied two ends of the scarf around her neck and the other two ends around her waist. The effect was amazing. In the front, the neckline dipped with seductive innocence, and the material gathered softly beneath her breasts. And as for the back, there was none.

Regarding the skirt, she had to admit that it fit her perfectly. Its hem hit her right above the knee, and the rich gold hue went perfectly with the colors in the scarf. She cast a dubious glance at her legs. She didn't own a pair of hose, and she hadn't had the money to buy any, so her long, ivory-toned legs were bare. She hoped no one would notice.

The knock on the door made her jump and press her hand over her wildly thumping heart. "Silly!" she snapped at the image in the mirror. For once in her life, she was dressed decently, fully prepared for the evening ahead!

But when she opened the door and saw the expression on Paul's face, all thoughts of cool composure vanished.

"You're beautiful," he said, his voice husky. "I'd like to stay right here and have you for dinner."

A warmth came up under ivory skin, tingeing it rose. It would be safer, she decided, not to respond to his remark, so she concentrated on him. Gold cuff links glinted at the French cuffs of his white shirt, and a subdued burgundy tie played against the navy blue of his suit. "Come in. You look very nice. But then I haven't seen you not look nice yet." *Understatement!* a voice in her head shouted.

He shut the door and leaned back against it. "Turn around."

Laughing nervously, she did as he requested. "I can't remember the last time I was dressed up like this."

Paul continued to stare at her. He'd always been fascinated by her green eyes, and tonight they shone brilliantly with a mixture of excitement and uncertainty.

And he'd always been entranced by her hair. From a center part, it fell in shimmering red waves down her bare back to below her shoulder blades. From where he stood, her ivory skin appeared smooth, soft, and infinitely touchable.

As he watched, she turned and her arm moved, causing the top she was wearing to shift slightly and expose the beginning swell of her breast from a side view. The slim gold skirt hugged the curve of her hips, tantalizing him with an indication of what was beneath. The high-heeled shoes on her feet added a graceful shapeliness to her long legs. The mere sight of her made his mouth go dry and his body harden. He wondered what effect touching her would have.

"Oh, Kathy," he murmured, "I'm going to have a tough time keeping my hands off you tonight." He pushed away from the door and took her into his arms. "In fact, it seems I can't resist you."

She joined her hands behind his neck and surrendered to his kiss without a murmur or a thought. There was no rhyme or reason to explain her feelings. They made no sense. All she knew was that she felt so right, so content in Paul's arms.

His hand stroked down her back, bringing heat and pleasurable sensations to the surface of her skin. His lips molded hers, pressing down with firm insistence, taking her toward passion with more force and speed than she had ever known before.

When her stomach growled, she ignored it and pressed closer to him. She wasn't at all ready to end this magical moment. When he pulled away from her, she frowned up at him. "What's wrong?"

"Did you eat lunch?"

"Lunch?" Her brow wrinkled with incomprehension. "I, uh, no, I don't think so."

"I know you didn't eat much breakfast, because you left most of the food on your plate."

Her back straightened defensively. "I told you I had already eaten."

"But that wasn't true, was it? And now, I'm willing to bet you're starving."

She was hungry, but she could never admit that to Paul. She bent her head as she stared at the floor, and her hair fell around her shoulders like a veil of fire.

With a finger under her chin, he tilted her face up. "I'm going to take you to one of the best restaurants in Dallas, and I want you to promise me you'll eat everything on your plate."

The heated sparks shimmering in his eyes, along with the concern in his voice made it impossible for her to resent his high-handed manner. Reluctantly, she smiled. "That won't be hard for me to do."

He nodded, satisfied. "Good." He bent and pressed his lips to hers. "That's to tide me over until I can kiss you again."

"But, Paul"—her voice was as soft as a sigh—"you're always kissing me."

He smiled. "That's right."

Paul astounded Kathy by driving them to the restaurant in a dark green Jaguar sedan. "I didn't know you could drive!"

"I'm from California."

"Okay. That explains why you don't have a Texas accent, but what has it got to do with driving?"

He laughed. "You can't get anywhere in California without driving, Kathy. All those freeways, you know."

"So why do you have Robert? And the limousine?"

"It frees me up. In the time it takes to drive from place to place, I can do a lot of work."

"I suppose so," she murmured, then lapsed into thoughtfulness. The reminder that Paul was an important man didn't come as a surprise. What did was that she was beginning to take the fact for granted.

The restaurant was as Kathy had predicted—elegant and exclusive. The waiters seemed to float among the tables without making the slightest sound. And discreet chamber music punctuated the delicate mood as it drifted from some undisclosed location.

Kathy put aside the menu. She assumed Paul's menu had the prices imprinted on it, since hers didn't, and decided it was a nice arrangement. One look might well give her a heart attack. But all the same, she knew she'd have no trouble at all fulfilling her promise to eat everything on her plate.

She glanced at Paul. He was consulting with the hovering waiter, discussing the pros and cons of various wines paired with different courses. All the wines and entrées had French names.

He looked up at her. "What do you think, Kathy?"

*Well*, she thought, *he asked*. "You know what I'd really like?"

Both men looked at her expectantly.

"A steak. I'd really love a big, juicy steak." From out of the corner of her eye she saw the waiter draw back in obvious horror, but Paul didn't even blink.

"That sounds good. I'll have the same." Paul sent a warning glance to the waiter while cursing himself. Why hadn't he realized that this wasn't the restaurant to bring her to? "And we want all the trimmings with that steak."

"Very good, sir. And the wine?"

In for a penny, in for a pound, Kathy thought. "Actually, I would really love some iced coffee."

"Iced coffee, miss?"

"Yes, please." She was already looking forward to it. Coffee was an item that was definitely too expensive to be on her shopping list.

"I'll just have water." Paul dismissed the waiter with a nod.

Kathy sat back with contentment. "I haven't had iced coffee since I left the East. This will be a real treat. And I can't remember the last time I had a—"

*"Paul!"* A melodious female voice interrupted her.

To Kathy, everything seemed to happen all at once. Paul's head turned. A huge smile spread across his face as he quickly stood. "Marissa!"

And then, much to her dismay, Paul's arms were enfolding the most beautiful woman Kathy had ever seen.

Masses of dark hair were twined into an elegant configuration at the base of her slender neck. Milky white skin gleamed through the exquisite black lace, haute couture creation she was wearing. And her amethyst eyes glittered at Paul with tenderness and intimacy.

"This is a great piece of luck running into you, Paul," the beautiful Marissa said in a soft Texas drawl, "because now I can yell at you in person!"

Kathy was sure Marissa had never yelled in her life. But Paul's response was even more interesting. His smile actually became sheepish.

"I've been meaning to call you."

Marissa laughed gaily, causing quite a few male heads to swivel in her direction. "Sure you have. And how many times have I heard that story?"

"Now, Marissa—"

"Don't you, *now, Marissa* me. By the way, you'll be glad to know that Beth Ann is worth every penny you're paying her. She's been coming up with some very creditable excuses for you. But I told her that if I didn't hear from you soon, I was going to call in the Texas Rangers."

"Yes, I got that message."

"I thought you would."

Kathy's dismay grew when the stunning amethyst eyes suddenly lit on her and a slender, white hand was extended toward her.

"Paul has deplorable manners for not introducing us. I'm Marissa Berryman."

Kathy took the offered hand. "I'm Kathy Broderick, and I think Paul has wonderful manners." To her surprise, approval lit up the jewel-toned eyes.

But Marissa's only comment was, "Well, well, Paul." before she turned to draw a man forward from the shadows behind her. "Kathy, this is Donald Spurgin."

Kathy nodded to the tall, handsome man who looked as if he had stepped out of a Neiman-Marcus ad for men's evening wear. Yet curiously, Kathy noticed that Marissa's whole demeanor seemed to harden and cool when she looked at Donald.

"Paul," Marissa asked, "have you met Donald?"

"No, I don't believe I have. How are you?"

"I'm fine, and it's a pleasure to meet you finally. You're practically a legend in the Dallas business community. I'd love the opportunity to talk to you." Donald glanced at his watch. "Unfortunately, though, we have to be on our way, or we'll be late."

"We're going to a benefit," Marissa explained to Kathy. "This town runs on benefits. Paul, I believe you were invited to this one?"

Paul gave her a serene smile. "I've made other plans."

"Good for you. By the way, have you made up your mind yet when you'll be leaving this year?"

A strange expression crossed his face. "No, I haven't."

Marissa placed her hand on his arm. "Then call me tomorrow, Thursday at the latest."

He covered her hand with his and bent to kiss her cheek. "I will. I promise."

"Kathy, it was a pleasure meeting you. I hope we have a chance to meet again."

Kathy wanted to dislike the exotic, amethyst-eyed Marissa, but for some reason she found it impossible. "I hope so, too," she murmured.

When the couple had left, Paul sat back down. "Sorry about the interruption, but Marissa's an old friend. I hope you didn't mind."

"Not at all. You say she's an old friend?" She hoped she was being tactful, but she was dying to know the nature of Marissa and Paul's relationship.

"Marissa was my wife's best friend. Since Sarah's death, Marissa and I have grown very close."

"You mean, you and she have, uh . . ."

Paul reached over and took her hand. "We've never been anything but friends, and we've never wanted to be. Over the years, Marissa and I both needed a good friend much more than we needed someone who would turn out to be just another lover. She had a short, bad marriage that left her very bitter toward men. She's often called the Ice Queen of Dallas society. Those of us who really know her, though, adore her."

"What about Donald?"

He shook his head. "Just another in a long line of men who think they can break through to her. The problem is, after what that bastard she married did to her, I'm not sure she'll ever trust another man."

"That's a shame." She thought for a minute. "What was that about your leaving this year? Where are you going?"

To Kathy's surprise, Paul's mouth tightened, but the appearance of the waiter temporarily stopped any more conversation. The waiter placed a glass filled with ice in front of Kathy, then proceeded to pour steaming hot coffee into the glass.

She couldn't hide her shock. "What are you doing?"

"Your iced coffee, miss."

"No, no, stop! You're going to break the glass! That's not how you make iced coffee!"

The waiter appeared genuinely perplexed. "How else would you make it?"

"You need to brew a pot of extra strong coffee, let it cool to room temperature, and *then* you pour it over ice." She rubbed her forehead, then smiled at him. "Never mind. You tried, and I really appreciate it. I'll just have water with dinner and a cup of coffee afterwards." When the young man left, Kathy shot Paul an amused look. "I keep forgetting I'm in Texas."

"I wish you wouldn't."

Her heart picked up an extra beat at the softness of his tone. "I just meant that in New York or Connecticut, no one would think twice if I ordered iced coffee."

"And it would probably be snowing outside, right?"

She smiled. "I do tend to go on about snow, don't I?"

"Are you really so homesick, Kathy?"

"I'm not sure if homesick is the right word. I like the Dallas area. I really do. It's simply that—"

"Things have been a struggle for you."

She was a bit unsettled over his perceptiveness. "That's right."

"Things will work out. I know they will."

She nodded in agreement. All her life she'd worked hard and made her own breaks. Now she had something of her very own—the shop—and *somehow* she was going to *make* things work out. *Somehow* she was going to convince the real estate company that this rent hike was totally unreasonable.

But all of her problems were separate from Paul, and for now she attempted to banish them from her mind. When the food came, she began to enjoy the meal without constraint. Paul was an entertaining dinner companion, and by the time her plate was clean, she couldn't remember having ever laughed so hard or eaten so much. She even chose a delicacy from the dessert cart, a large slice of apple pie with praline crust and crème glacé topping.

"I think I've gained ten pounds tonight," she said, groaning as she unlocked the door of her apartment. She'd invited Paul to come in for a while, but she was still somewhat nervous.

"You could afford to gain twenty-five pounds without anyone noticing." He sank down onto the sofa.

"I have several pairs of jeans that would notice. Like old friends, we're used to each other just the way we are."

Paul's presence somehow made her apartment seem even smaller. She was standing almost in the kitchen area, a good ten feet away from him, but his blue-eyed gaze was intense and probing. Last night she'd been preoccupied by the pain of her headache. Tonight there was nothing to distract her from the sensual magnetism of the man. She looked around the apartment, searching for something to do or say. "I'm afraid I have nothing to serve you."

"After that meal, I don't need anything . . . except you. Come sit with me."

She paused, wondering where she should sit. Then he grabbed her hand and pulled her down close beside him.

From the first meeting, their relationship had been unorthodox, and tonight was no exception. Preliminaries were not for them.

His hand smoothed back her hair. "I want you, Kathy."

"I know." And she also knew something else. She was tumbling headlong into love with him, and there was nothing she could do to stop herself. Shadows lay thick around them as she relaxed, her body softening against him.

His palm skimmed up and down her spine, searing the bare flesh. His other hand tangled in her hair, holding her head in place for his mouth to ravish. Thick, sweet heat curled around her insides like a rippling stream of liquid fire.

"Come close," he murmured against her mouth.

"I can't get any closer," she whispered, trying all the same. The need to give herself up to the kiss was intense and undeniable, and she twisted against him. With each movement, the silk of her skirt rode higher up her thigh.

"I need you closer!"

Deft fingers worked open the scarf's knot at her waist, then slipped around her ribcage until he could take the fullness of her into his hand. She moaned even as she clung to him, and Paul felt the muscles in his stomach harden. His thumb found the stiff nub of her nipple, and raw desire burned through his blood like a raging fire.

It would destroy him if he didn't have her soon. He couldn't get enough of her into his hands to satisfy him. He couldn't get his tongue deep enough into her mouth. And once he was inside her, would he be able to move fast enough, drive hard enough? Would he ever get enough of this woman? Or would he just have to keep making love to her forever?

Kathy felt lost in satin-soft, fiery-hot sensations. His need for her came through every stroke of his hands along her skin. Making love with Paul for the first time would be the most important event of her life, she decided. She'd have no bruises in the morning, only wonderful memories.

Every muscle in Paul's body was straining for control, every cell was aflame with his passion. One of his hands went to the silky smoothness of her thigh and glided upward. The other went to the knot at her neck. Soon . . .

Kathy groaned as a sharp pain knifed through her stomach. Then another pain followed, and another, until her whole stomach was gripped. She wrapped her arms over her abdomen and folded forward.

"My God, Kathy, what's wrong?"

"My stomach's cramping." Her words came out in labored puffs, and she could feel perspiration breaking out on her forehead. "I should have been . . . more careful. I'm not used to eating . . . so much at once." Embarrassed beyond belief, she closed her eyes.

Paul uttered a curse. "Dammit, Kathy, you've been starving! I saw what was in your refrigerator. The damned mice are probably eating better than you."

"Could you . . . just help me to . . . the bedroom and yell at me . . . later?"

He swept her into his arms and carried her to bed. It didn't take him long to strip off her clothes. Rifling her drawers, he found an oversized T-shirt that said *Simon and Garfunkel.* He slipped it over her head and settled her beneath the covers.

"I don't suppose you have any Alka-Seltzer?"

"No."

"Pepto-Bismol? Club soda?"

"No." She turned onto her side and curled into a fetal position, wishing she could suddenly become invisible.

'No, of course not. Why would I think you'd have medicine when you don't even have any food!"

"I have a heating pad in the closet. My mother

. . . insisted." Of the three things she was feeling —embarrassment, humiliation, and stomach pain —she'd choose the stomach pain any day. Paul had been taking care of her continuously since he'd met her. No man would put up with that. She was going to lose him before she ever had him.

Silently he plugged in the heating pad and handed it to her. "I'm going out to see if I can find a drugstore that's still open. You need some medicine. Will you be all right until I return?"

"I'll be fine, but there's no need for you to come back. In fact, I wish you wouldn't."

Despondency threaded her voice. She didn't see his tender smile, but she felt his good-bye kiss on her cheek.

"Just rest, Kathy."

"I will."

In a moment she heard her front door close behind him and knew that she was alone. A sudden exhaustion overcame her. She felt completely drained, both emotionally and physically. Too much had happened too quickly. Tomorrow, she decided, she'd deal with everything. For now, she let the heat gradually sooth and relax the tight muscles of her stomach. It wasn't long before she drifted off to sleep.

Some time later, Paul let himself in the door, carrying a bag of groceries and over-the-counter medications for everything from sinus trouble to stomach pains. After checking on Kathy and seeing that she was asleep, he made ten trips up and down the stairs, carrying the rest of his purchases. It took him two more hours to sort and put everything away. When he was finished, the refrigerator and freezer were packed with food, and the cupboards were filled with canned goods, boxed cereal, rice, and pasta, as was the small closet that served as a pantry. He stacked the overflow on the floor and on top of the counters.

When he was finished, he tiptoed into the bedroom and pressed a soft kiss to Kathy's cheek. "If you think a little stomachache is going to make me go away, you're wrong," he whispered.

And then, before he bedded down on the couch, he put out a small wedge of cheese for the mice.

## Four

When Kathy awakened the next morning, she felt slightly disoriented. Something didn't seem right. Her hand moved fretfully and encountered the heating pad on her stomach. With a groan, she opened her eyes, and memories of the night before came flooding back to her, memories she would have just as soon forgotten.

A stomachache! *Way to go, Kathy. Real romantic!* She pressed the heels of her hands against her eyes, reliving the embarrassment of the night before.

Gradually noises seeped into her consciousness, noises that sounded as if they were coming from her kitchen. As she struggled to sit up, the bedroom door opened, and a cheerful Paul strolled in.

"Well, good morning! How's your tummy?"

Pushing a handful of hair out of her eyes, Kathy viewed him with astonishment. The white dress shirt he was wearing was completely unbuttoned and hanging free over a pair of wrinkled dark blue trousers. They were the same clothes he had worn the night before! "Paul, what are you doing here?"

"I'm asking you how you feel. Didn't you hear my question?"

She made a quick, impatient wave with her hand. "I'm fine. I simply ate too much last night, that's all."

His smile disappeared, and he sat down beside her on the bed. "What you mean is, last night, for the first time in a long time, you had a full meal."

The anger in his voice came through to her loud and clear, and she couldn't blame him one bit. Any man would be angry under the same circumstances. Last night, she had fallen in love with him. And she would have made love with him, except . . . She supposed their interrupted lovemaking could be chalked up to the laws of nature.

"I'm sorry about last night, Paul. You have every right to be mad." She lowered her eyes to his chest, wanting to hide her dismay and sadness. "In the short time you've known me, you've had to nurse me through a cut forehead, a headache, and a stomachache. It's not terribly romantic, is it? I mean, we were . . . we almost . . . I mean . . ." A finger lifted her chin so that she was forced to look at him.

"Do you honestly think that's why I'm angry? Because we didn't make love? Kathy, I want you, make no mistake about that, and we'll have many more nights like last night. I'm warning you, though. Last night was the last time you'll be sick from starving yourself."

Pride made her defensive. "That's not true! I haven't been starving myself!"

"Don't lie to me. You had nothing in your cupboards or refrigerator."

She tried to make her shrug nonchalant. "So you caught me between shopping trips."

"I said, *don't lie to me.*"

Her habits of self-reliance died hard. "Oatmeal and peanut butter are very nutritious. As a matter of fact, oatmeal can be a great help in reducing levels of cholesterol, and peanut butter is a wonderful source of protein."

She expected more anger, more arguments. Instead, she received a kiss that disarmed her completely. He pressed his lips to hers with a fervent warmth that was hard to resist. She rested her hands on his shoulders and touched the warm column of his neck with her fingers. No matter what she did or said, he seemed to know the precise buttons to push to make her dissolve into a blob of jelly. Clearly he'd had a lot of experience with women.

Paul didn't love her; he wanted her. The laws of nature covered this situation with clarity. An affair between them would be very short, and she'd be left with a broken heart.

Floating along on a river of pleasure, she decided that, somehow, she had to find a way to neutralize the effect of his power over her. "Paul . . ."

"Save your breath for kissing me," he murmured against her mouth, "because you're never going to convince me that you've been eating a well-balanced diet. You haven't been able to eat enough or the right kinds of foods because you've been trying to save money. Am I right?"

She jerked her chin out of his hold. "Let it go, will you? I've been doing fine up until now, thank you very much!" Her words were uttered from between clenched teeth. "What's more, what I eat or don't eat is none of your business. And in addition, you never answered my question. What are you doing here?"

"I spent the night here."

That took the wind out of her sails. "You *what?*"

He nodded, unperturbed at her indignation. "On your couch. There was no way I was going to leave you alone in pain. I wanted to be available in case you woke up in the night and needed something. Would you like a cup of coffee?"

"I don't have any coffee."

"I'll get you some in a minute. But first I want you to promise me something. By the way, I love the way you look when you first wake up, all soft and dreamy. I'm going to see you that way a lot." His voice had lowered, softened, as if his words were stroking her skin with a piece of velvet.

"You want me to promise you something?" she prompted.

"I want you to promise that from now on you will eat at least three sensible meals a day. I want you to be healthy, happy, and wise."

Irritated, she raked her fingers through her hair. "You're never going to believe me, but I'm rarely sick."

His hand lightly skimmed up and down her arm. "How long have you been cutting corners on food?"

"Since I've had the shop. About seven months."

"I guarantee you, if you'd continued the way you were going, you would have been sick before the winter was over."

She just might have a chance to resist him, she thought crossly, if he didn't always seem to be touching her. "I'm very hardy!"

He slipped his hand beneath the short, loose sleeve of her T-shirt and circled her upper arm until his thumb and fingers almost met. "You're about as hardy as a baby bird. I'm a selfish man, Kathy. I want you in my arms and in my bed. Fit and very active."

Her blood was heating, and she could think of nothing that could cool it. Perhaps reality would sober him up. "Paul, this is never going to work."

His smile thwarted her strategy. "Believe that for as long as you can, Kathy. But also believe this. You're going to be mine."

He bent forward, but instead of kissing her, he took her bottom lip between his teeth. Gently his teeth grated back and forth across the sensitive tissue, bringing delicate nerve endings to life. She raised her hands to his shoulders and wasn't at all surprised to hear a faint moan of desire come from her throat. Dammit, but she did want him so.

Slowly her mouth parted. His tongue accepted the invitation and plunged into the waiting heat. Beneath the T-shirt, her breasts were aching, and even though she said nothing, he seemed to know of her need. His hand slipped under the T-shirt and closed around her, making her shudder.

"I didn't mean to make love to you this morning," he murmured. "I only planned to cook breakfast for you."

"Just kiss me," she breathed. "That's all I want."

"I want more than that."

She clung to him, ready and willing for what was to come. Paul didn't know that she loved him, but that made no difference. Her love for him was now a solid part of her. It wasn't something she could take back or exchange like an article of clothing that didn't fit. Nor was her love for him something that she could throw away or deny.

No, her love for Paul would be with her always. And when he pulled her down in the bed and pushed her T-shirt over her head, she eagerly helped. Passion was building within her, a passion so intense, she wasn't sure what to do. How did one survive such a powerful experience? *Did* one survive?

Paul caught one erect nipple between his lips and tugged, then took it fully into his mouth. He hadn't planned this, he thought, but he couldn't stop it, either. The feeling of possessiveness was strong within him. He'd been to bed with a number of women since Sarah had died, but the attraction had been purely physically. Kathy was different, although he didn't know how and he didn't know why. He only knew that he wanted her, and he was going to have her.

All his senses were alive. Mental images were intensified and seemed to stand in relief. An incredible energy filled the air that he was breathing. The clock beside the bed ticked too fast, yet too slow. Amazingly, the morning light that shone through the window illuminated only their entwined bodies and cast the rest of the room in shadows.

He was incapable of being apart from her for the short length of time it would take for him to finish undressing. So he shrugged out of his shirt and opened his pants.

Exploring, his mouth went lower, nibbling past her navel until it encountered the elastic lace of her panties, riding low on her hips. They were no barrier at all. Pushing the fabric down, he continued toward the sweetness.

Kathy felt his fingers delve between her legs and into her softness. Pleasure unequal to anything she'd ever known flared into her like tiny comets. "Ah . . . Paul . . . I'm melting."

He laughed softly and finished stripping off her panties. "I told you I was going to find your exact melting point. Next time it will be a different point." He was stroking her, making erotic patterns with his fingers. "Perhaps next time that point will come quicker . . . and will feel even better."

She exhaled raggedly. "Impossible."

"No, it's not. Each time will be better. I promise you."

Passion and pressure were one and the same in her. "What's happening?"

"Something wonderful. Kathy . . . I can't wait any longer."

Her hands moved to his buttocks, urgently. "Don't. Please don't wait."

He raised himself up and gently entered her. She wanted him so badly, she didn't even think about tensing up, and because of that, there was no pain.

Still he was careful. He went deeper into her, little by little, and as he did, bursts of fiery pleasure started going off inside her. By the time he had completely filled her, her head was thrown back and she was gasping. "Paul! You were right! It *was* wonderful!"

"Just wait." He ground out the words and began to thrust.

With reluctance, Kathy forced herself to open her eyes. She was lying on her side, and she could feel Paul behind her, his body curved around hers. A sudden thought made her groan. "Oh, my word! What time is it? I've got to go to work!"

He lifted his head and rested his cheek on her hair. "It's early yet. Not quite seven-thirty. What time do you open your shop?"

"Officially the store doesn't open until ten." Wondering if the happiness she felt would be reflected in her eyes, she rolled over on her back and gazed up at him. "That's when all the other shops in the village open. But I usually get there around eight to work on the stock. When early-bird customers happen by, you can bet I don't turn them away."

"Well, this morning, you're not going to get there quite so early. First we're going to take a shower, and then we're going to eat a nutritious breakfast."

"Oatmeal?"

He smiled down at her and gathered her to him. "You know what I think?"

"What?" she asked dutifully.

"I think the shower and breakfast can wait for a little while." He took a gentle nip of her ear. "What do you think?"

"I suppose they can." His lips were making their way down the side of her throat. Under the circumstances, she decided, getting to the shop just a little later than normal wouldn't hurt. Then she remembered. This morning she *had* to go to the real estate company. "Oh, gosh . . . Paul, I'm sorry, but I've got to get up now."

He raised himself up on his elbow, a rueful expression on his face. "This isn't very good for my ego, you know."

She laughed lightly. "I'm sorry. It's just that I have something really important to do today."

"I like it when you laugh," he murmured.

She screwed her face into a mock scowl. "You're deliberately trying to make it hard for me to get out of this bed."

"I admit nothing." In a sudden move, he jumped out of bed and reached for her.

She made a sound that was a cross between a squeal and a laugh. "What are you doing?"

"Making it easy for you to get out of bed." He swung her up in his arms and headed for the bathroom. Once there, he deposited her on her feet in the tub, got in with her, and turned on the water.

Within a short time, they were lathering each other's bodies with loving care and attention. Deliciously warm water sprayed over them, and the sweet, clean smell of the soap invaded their pores. Just when Kathy thought her legs wouldn't support her another minute, Paul sat down in the tub, and pulled her onto his lap. With him deep inside her and her moving against him, they provided their own heat, and didn't even notice when the hot water turned cool.

• • •

As she dressed, Kathy could hear the sounds of Paul cooking breakfast in her kitchen. Since she'd had to blow-dry her hair, she was a little slower in leaving the bedroom than he had been. Pulling on her jeans, she tried to remember if she had any milk in the refrigerator. She'd eaten oatmeal many times by itself, but somehow she doubted if Paul would find the prospect too appetizing.

She passed a mirror and caught sight of the silly grin that was plastered on her face. *So much for the laws of nature!* She and Paul would just have to make up their own laws. Extremely pleased with this new conclusion, she grabbed a moss green pullover out of the bureau drawer and tugged it over her head.

"Kathy! Breakfast is ready."

"I'll be right there!" she called. Pulling her hair from beneath the sweater and flicking it over her shoulders, she started down the short hall that led to the kitchen. "Boy, this is a treat. I'm not used to being waited—" Her voice died away as she tried to absorb the sight before her. Groceries were everywhere! On the floor. On the table. On the counter. On top of the refrigerator. "Paul, what *is* all this?"

"Do you remember last night when I went out to get you some medicine?"

She nodded numbly.

"Well, all the drugstores were closed, but I did find a supermarket. So as long as I was there, I bought a few other things."

"A *few* other things, Paul?"

He set a dish of scrambled eggs on the little

kitchen table and went to her. "I couldn't stand the thought of you without enough food. Don't make a big deal out of it."

She swept her arm out. "But there must be hundreds of dollars worth of groceries here! How am I ever going to be able to pay you back for all of this?"

"I don't want you to pay me back. I want you to eat the food in good health."

She crossed her arms over her chest. "Paul, you've been feeding me ever since you first met me!"

"Someone had to."

"Dammit!" Suddenly she grinned. "You're as stubborn as I am, aren't you? We could go back and forth for hours on this subject and never agree."

"So you'll accept the food."

It wasn't a question, but she didn't accept his statement as law, either.

"I can't see the supermarket taking all of this back, but"—she chewed thoughtfully on a thumbnail—"I suppose I can make a note of each item as I use it, and then I could pay you back a little at a time."

He pulled her hand away from her mouth. "No way. I know you. You won't eat the food unless you think you can afford it, and since you can't afford it, you'll starve yourself again rather than accept my help."

She peered up at him through her lashes. "The only way I'll consider eating any of this food is if you'll help me."

He relaxed his grip on her. "Is that an invitation to dinner tonight?"

"Absolutely." And every meal thereafter, she thought, but because he hadn't spoken of love, she remained quiet on the subject of their future. For now, dinner tonight was enough.

He smiled down at her with satisfaction. "Great, then let's have breakfast. Making love with you has left me ravenous!"

Kathy chained her bicycle to a parking meter, then turned to gaze up at the Hayes Building, an elegant structure of concrete, glass, and steel. The man she'd spoken to at the real estate company had given her detailed directions. He'd also mentioned that the Hayes Building was one of the older skyscrapers in downtown Dallas. If that was the case, Kathy decided, the building wore its years well.

At the real estate company, she had learned that Bluebonnet Village had been bought by the Hayes Corporation, which was part of the Steele Corporation. Since her college curriculum had included so many business courses, she knew all about the Steele Corporation and its formidable chairman of the board, James Steele. Now that she knew who and what she was up against, her confidence was ebbing. The rental of her shop was such a minor cog in the giant wheel of a network like the Steele Corporation.

But with or without confidence, she had no choice, she reminded herself grimly. She had to try. Quickly she combed through her hair with her fingers, attempting to undo the disheveled effects of the wind. Then she entered the building.

Minutes later, she was on the thirty-fifth floor, which housed the executive offices of the Hayes Corporation. Having slipped past the receptionist and two other secretaries, she found herself being given the once-over by a very attractive and very pregnant executive assistant. The nameplate on the woman's desk read: BETH ANN MARKOVICH.

"And you say you don't have an appointment?"

"No." Kathy cast a longing glance at the unmarked door behind the woman. "And my name wouldn't mean anything to the president, either. But if I could just have a moment of his time, I would be forever grateful."

"Perhaps if you could give me an idea of what this concerns, I might be able to help you."

"I wish you could, but I'm afraid only the president of the company will be able to help me."

"I see. What is your name?"

"Kathy Broderick."

Beth Ann tapped her pencil thoughtfully against her desk. She'd been Paul Garth's assistant for eight years, ever since Skye Anderson had resigned her position as secretary to Jonathan Hayes and married the new owner of the company, James Steele. It wasn't Beth Ann's practice to let strangers into Paul's office without an appointment, but there was something about this young woman that was very compelling.

Beth Ann rested a hand on the convenient shelf of her stomach, the result of eight months of pregnancy, and contemplated Kathy Broderick. She certainly wasn't Paul's typical visitor. Maybe that was why she felt an instant sympathy and compassion toward the red-haired young woman. Or maybe it was the hint of desperation she detected in the beautiful green eyes that touched a chord somewhere inside her. She smiled ruefully to herself. Well, whatever it was, Beth Ann was going to try to get Paul to see the young woman.

She placed her hands flat on her desk and pushed herself upright. "He's going to kill me."

"I beg your pardon?"

"Nothing," Beth Ann said smoothly. "I was just muttering to myself. Something I'm afraid I do quite a bit lately. If you'll just have a seat, I'll go see what I can do for you."

"Oh, thank you so much!"

The smile that lit up Kathy's face made Beth Ann all the more determined, but she held up a warning finger. "I can't promise anything."

"I understand." Too nervous to sit, Kathy crossed her fingers and began to pace. This had to work!

Beth Ann's feet sank into the thick carpeting as she crossed the spacious office. Paul's desk sat in the center of the large room. There was a conference table with phones and chairs to the left. To the right, a semicircular grouping of sofas and chairs provided a comfortable conversational area. Beyond that was an oval pecan dining room table. And at the very end of the room, a door led to a small, but very efficient kitchen.

She had recently supervised the redecoration of the office in shades of cream, brown, teal, and green, and Beth Ann was quite pleased with the effect.

"Paul, there's someone outside waiting to see you."

He'd been standing by a wall of glass, gazing out over the view of downtown Dallas and the plains beyond. When he turned to her, the expression on his face revealed his preoccupation. "I didn't know I had an appointment now."

"You don't. Not exactly." She stopped at his desk and automatically began straightening things. "It's just that this extraordinary young woman showed up, wanting to see you."

"Did she say what she wanted?"

"No, but I get the impression it's very important."

Paul chuckled. "I think your pregnancy has made you go soft, Beth Ann. For eight years, you've guarded me like a mother dragon. And now suddenly you want me to see a total stranger who probably just wants money for some new charity? That husband of yours had better watch out, or you'll be bringing home all sorts of strays, and then you won't have room for the baby when he or she finally decides to show its beautiful face."

A warm glow spread over Beth Ann at the mention of her husband, Drake, and their baby. When Beth Ann first met Paul, she'd developed a mad crush on him, but it had taken only one smile from Drake a few months later to show her what real love was all about. "Paul, I really think—"

He held up his hand. "I don't have the time or the patience today. Listen to her story, and if you think it's worthwhile, write her a check." He sat down at his desk and pulled a sheaf of papers toward him. "Have the jet standing by late this evening. James called earlier and wants me to fly out for a couple of days. There's a company out there he wants my opinion on."

Beth Ann smiled. "I miss Skye. I wish I wasn't so far along that I couldn't travel. I'd take a few days off and go with you."

"I'm sure as soon as you have that baby, she'll be flying in."

"Probably. But I wish they didn't live so far away. I'd like to see her more than the five or six times a year we've been averaging."

Paul grinned. "James and Skye. We miss them, but those two need no one but each other."

"That's true."

She'd turned and was halfway across the room, when something clicked in Paul's head. "Wait a minute. Why do you think the young woman waiting to see me is so extraordinary?"

"I don't really know. There's just something about her."

"I assume she gave you a name?"

"Kathy Broderick."

Paul was out of his chair and across the room before Beth Ann knew what was happening. He jerked open the door. "Kathy?"

She whirled toward the sound of the familiar voice in surprise. "Paul?"

Immediately, he approached her, a big smile on his face. "Why didn't you tell me you were coming?"

"How could I have done that?" she asked dumbly, not sure she wanted to believe what she was seeing.

He took her hands in his. "I gave you my card when we first met. Remember? You look wonderful! Your cheeks have some color. All that food I've been shoveling into you is paying off."

"The wind put the color into my cheeks." Her reply was automatic. She was staring at the unmarked door behind him. "Do you mean to tell me that *you're* the president of the Hayes Corporation?"

"Yes, of course. Didn't you realize that?" He ushered her past an amazed Beth Ann and into his office.

"How could I have realized?" Indignation was rapidly replacing her surprise.

"My card, Kathy. My card. Didn't you even look at it?" He laughed, incredibly happy to see her. She'd been in his thoughts all morning, and his need for her had been a steady, growing thing. As soon as the door was shut behind them, he drew her into his arms.

She didn't want to respond to his kiss, but finding him here had knocked her completely off balance. While her mind was busy trying to make sense of things, her body reacted. Without wanting to, she softened against him. Without intending to, she parted her lips for him. And when he ended the kiss, she had to struggle to regain her composure.

"Lord, but I'm glad to see you." His laugh was soft and deep. "I've been away from you for just a few hours, and I was ready to climb the walls."

She pushed away from him. Only then did he notice the distressed look on her face. "What's the matter, Kathy?"

She drew a hard, painful breath into her lungs. "I had no idea you were the president of this company."

He studied her, trying to find some clue as to why he suddenly felt so uneasy. "Something's happening here, but I don't know what it is."

There were various reasons for Kathy's distress. For one thing, the big bad president raising her rent was Paul. Paul, the same man she'd made love with just a few hours earlier. She needed to remain cool and logical in her discussion with him, but how could she when her heart was breaking?

And why in the world hadn't she thought to ask Paul what he had been doing in Bluebonnet Village that morning two days ago? *Not very smart, Kathy. Not very smart at all.*

In addition, she felt as if there were DO NOT TOUCH signs everywhere in this luxurious office in the sky. She was way out of her league here. On the other hand, Paul looked completely at home.

"This office is as big as my shop," she murmured, taking in the gleaming teak desk that seemed as long as a banquet table.

"Not quite. Come sit down. I'll have Beth Ann bring us something to drink."

*Beth Ann.* Kathy closed her eyes, annoyed at herself. Of course. Now she remembered that Marissa had said something about a Beth Ann to Paul.

"What would you like?" He had the receiver in his hand. "I'll order lunch for us."

She sank into a chair in front of the desk. "No, please, I couldn't eat a thing." It was true. She felt as if there were a fist embedded in her stomach.

He set the receiver back into its cradle and leaned against the edge of the desk to consider her. She had mentioned that the wind was responsible for the color in her cheeks. More than likely it was also responsible for the charming disarray of her hair as it streamed and curled over the green sweater. "You rode your bicycle over here, didn't you?"

His tone of censure made her quickly lift her head. "How else do you think I could have gotten here?"

"Robert will drive you anywhere you want to go, including here."

"Robert's your driver, not mine."

"You could have been hurt in all that traffic. Don't you have any sense of self-preservation?"

"Evidently not." The bite in her words was ominous.

He sighed. "Okay, okay, I think we'd better drop the subject for now. I guess I should be grateful it wasn't cold and raining."

"In Dallas? Are you kidding?"

Wondering why she was so angry, he ignored her sarcasm. "I'm glad to see you, Kathy. But if you didn't know who I was, why are you here?"

Her heart was cold. From their first encounter, she'd known that Paul was a man of authority and command. In her own way, she'd been struggling with that fact, and in her own way, she'd been coming to terms with it. But seeing him in this milieu, she felt alienated and shocked.

Aside from all of that, though, one harsh reality sent a piercing, chilling pain through her heart: Paul was the man responsible for raising the rent of her shop! *Now he was a part of her problem instead of being separate from it.*

"Kathy?"

There was only one option left for her, she decided. She had to say her piece as quickly as possible and then leave. She drew the folded letter out of her jeans pocket and handed it to him.

"I received this letter day before yesterday from a real estate firm, informing me that the rent on my shop would be raised five hundred dollars. This morning, I went over there to tell them that I couldn't possibly afford that. They informed me that they were just following orders, *your* orders, it now turns out."

A look of genuine shock crossed his face. "Damn! I forgot all about this! Lord, Kathy, I'm sorry, but if you received the letter day before yesterday, why haven't you mentioned it to me before now?"

"At the time, I didn't think it was anything that concerned you!" Was she really snapping at the very man she had intended to sway over to her side? Now was not the time to let her personal doubts and disappointments intrude, she reminded herself. And she absolutely had to forget the fire of his lovemaking! This was business!

"Paul, five hundred dollars is an outrageous increase. I'm sure you'll agree. Actually, *any* increase at this time is out of the question. You've seen Bluebonnet Village. You must have noticed how run-down it is."

"Kathy, I knew it was run-down before I ever saw it. Bill Ludlow is my vice president in charge of real estate. He prepared extensive reports on the village before I ever gave the go-ahead for the buy."

"Then you must understand!" Unconsciously,

she sat forward. "Remember when I had such a headache, and I rambled on about my shop? I think I told you that I fell in love with it because the village resembled a place that time had passed by. Maybe I was too naive. The charm of the place and the low rent won me over. I guess I should have realized all that could change. Although I've struggled to make a go of the shop, nothing ever made me feel that the situation was hopeless. At least, not until I got that letter."

The distress in her voice was hard for Paul to bear. He silently cursed himself for not having taken care of this mess before it reached this point. Intending to pull her into his arms, he reached for her, but she jerked violently away.

"I came to see the president of the Hayes Corporation. Please keep that in mind!"

Paul folded his arms across his chest and slowly exhaled. She was too stubborn for her own good! "Okay, Kathy. We'll play it your way, for now, at any rate. And I'll give you the bottom line first. We weren't buying the shops. We were buying the buildings. If tenants have to move, new ones will move in. That's the way it always goes in situations like this.

"In the case of Bluebonnet Village, Bill Ludlow estimated that half of the tenants wouldn't be hurt by the increase. They've been there for years and have made enough money to see them through until we put our plans into effect. I gave the okay based on his reports. I didn't actually visit the village until the morning I met you. But even if I knew that every single one of the tenants would have to relocate to a cheaper location, it wouldn't have affected my decision. That's business. It happens every day."

The cold-blooded truth of his statement sent chills through her.

Paul came away from the desk, pulled a chair next to hers, and sat down. "Bluebonnet Village hasn't made a profit for its owners in several years now. That's why we were able to pick it up for such a good price. The owners let the village fall into disrepair, and the people in the surrounding areas have forgotten that it's even there."

Without thinking about what he was doing, he shifted closer to her, willing her to understand. "The rent increase is totally in line with what other businesses in the surrounding areas are paying. Now, those other stores are doing excellent business, and there's no reason why the shops in the village can't do as well. You must know that a large portion of that area is affluent. The Hayes Corporation has developed a renovation and advertising campaign aimed toward that upscale market. Once it's under way, every shop in the village will have more business than ever before. With that kind of profit, the tenants will have no problem paying higher rent, believe me."

Kathy had listened very carefully. Everything he said made sense. But none of it helped her. "I'm sure that all looks wonderful on paper. But what about the reality? What about between now and the time when all of this business is supposed to pour into our shops? And what if you're wrong and the business doesn't come?"

"I'm not wrong, Kathy. I'm very good at this, or I wouldn't be employed by the Steele Corporation.

And, by the way, rent increases are standard procedure when we buy a new piece of property that we plan to sink a great deal of money into. I didn't know the letters had gone out yet, but then it's not normally something that would be brought to my attention."

Suddenly Paul tired of playing the corporate president. The worried look evident in the softness of her emerald eyes tore at him. He reached over and took both her hands. "Look, this is all my fault. I've been so busy trying to feed you, it didn't occur to me to think much about your shop. We should have talked abut this before now. I was just thinking of other things."

"You don't have to explain." She flushed, knowing what he had been thinking of.

When she tried to withdraw her hands, his grip tightened. "I don't want you worrying about this. You don't have to pay the five hundred extra dollars until the renovation is completed and the new customers start coming in. As a matter of fact, now that I think about it, I'll suspend your rent altogether until you can get the shop on its feet." As soon as he saw the color disappear from her face, he knew he'd made a serious mistake.

Anger and pain warred within her, and Kathy felt herself begin to shake. Paul couldn't have said anything more insulting to her if he'd tried. "You told me right up front that you wanted me. So, of course, I know what I've done—or perhaps more to the point, what you expect me to do in the future—to earn this largess from you."

"Kathy, you're misinterpreting my gesture. I've seen how hard you're trying to hold things together, and I admire what you're doing. I just want to help you, that's all."

"Enough to forget my rent for a while?"

"That's right."

How nice, Kathy thought dully. Except he wasn't mentioning the rent of the other tenants. But then, she reminded herself bitterly, it had been *she* that he'd spent the morning in bed with, not they.

"I'm afraid that I can't accept your very generous offer." It took every ounce of inner strength she possessed to move, but she forced herself to stand. "Now if you'll excuse me, I have a long ride back to my shop."

He jerked to his feet. "You can't leave like this, Kathy! We need to talk."

"I think we just have."

"Look, I've got to fly to California this evening. I had planned to invite you to go with me . . ."

"That's very thoughtful of you, but I've always considered California a foreign country, and I don't have a passport." She put a hand to her head. *Lord, what am I saying?* She had to get out of this office before she made an even bigger fool of herself! In the next moment she was horrified to hear herself saying, "You want to hear something that'll make you laugh? I fell in love with you! Can you beat that? Isn't that the funniest thing you ever heard?"

There. It was over. She'd said it.

A detached calm settled over her, and she watched curiously as the color drained out of his face.

*It's as if I cut him, and he's bleeding,* she thought, waiting for his response.

*What will I do if he tells me he loves me?* she wondered.

*What will I do if he says he doesn't love me?*

She hadn't considered the possibility that he might say nothing at all. But the silence stretched and stretched, until Kathy considered picking up the marble ashtray that was sitting on the corner of his desk and throwing it at the glass wall behind him. Even the crash of shattering glass would be better than this ominous silence.

"I'll be gone at least a couple of days," Paul finally said, as if something extraordinary hadn't just occurred. "When I get back—"

"No!" She couldn't bear any more. "I understand your position, and I hope you understand mine. I solve my own problems, Paul."

"And what if you can't?"

"If I can't, it's not your concern. Good bye."

He made no more effort to stop her from leaving. He couldn't. He waited until the door had closed behind her, then walked to his desk, and with a hand that was not quite steady, pushed a button on his intercom. "Beth Ann, I want to speak to Marissa Berryman. Then ask Bill Ludlow to come in."

# Five

Usually Kathy spent the evening working on ideas for upcoming displays, but that night she was hard put to summon even the most idle interest. Why bother planning future displays when she might have to put her shop up for sale tomorrow? she asked herself.

The shop had been her world until Paul had come along, and she had tumbled into love with him with all the innocence of a young girl. The reality was that at twenty-six she wasn't a young girl, and she should have known better.

In retrospect, it would have been much simpler if she'd fallen down Alice's rabbit hole instead of into Paul's limousine. Before that day, she'd only had one problem—making ends meet until her shop could get on its feet. Now she had another—her love for Paul and the fact that he didn't love her.

Trying to be fair, she acknowledged that he hadn't deliberately betrayed her. His company had bought the village, and the real estate company had sent the notifications out before she and Paul had even met. But when she'd found out that he was president of the Hayes Corporation, she'd been crushed. To know that he was the one destroying her dream was almost too much to bear. Perhaps it wasn't a reasonable or even practical way for her to look at the matter, but there it was. And there wasn't a thing she could do about it.

He'd offered help, but her damnable pride made it impossible for her to accept. Perhaps her sin was too much pride. If so, she consoled herself with the knowledge that perfection was not the strong suit of any member of the human race.

The facts before her were simple. She couldn't allow Paul or anyone else to feel sorry for her. If she couldn't find a way of saving her shop on her own, she'd have to sell it. She refused to let Toni take any more of a loss on her investment than was necessary.

She saved her other problem to consider last. She couldn't believe the way she'd blurted out her love to Paul, but she'd done it, and wishing for the words back wouldn't do her a bit of good. Nor would wishing that she could forget the hurt expression on his face when she'd told him. She'd take that memory with her to her grave. He'd looked . . . *wounded*. She didn't understand. But heartbreaking though it was, she would have to accept the fact that he didn't love her and get on with her life.

Kathy skipped dinner. The thought of how much

money she owed Paul for the food in her kitchen had her stomach turning. But the next morning, she forced herself to cook a hearty breakfast. No matter what happened, she was going to need strength—strength to help her come up with an idea to save her shop, or strength to help her endure the emotional trauma of losing it.

In all her plans, she left Paul completely out of the picture, because as far as she was concerned, he was. The laws of nature had struck again.

At the shop, she methodically went over column after column of figures, trying to see profit where there was only loss. About eleven o'clock, she received a special delivery letter from the real estate company. The letter stated that Mr. Bill Ludlow, vice president of the Hayes Corporation, had decided to waive the five-hundred-dollar increase for ten months.

Anger was Kathy's first response. No matter what the letter said, it was Paul Garth who was behind the decision. And *she* was the reason for his decision.

With his silence, he'd made it clear that he didn't love her. With this letter, he was making it clear that he still wanted her. The man was going to have to learn that he couldn't manipulate people, making them do whatever he wanted.

But as the day wore on, and Kathy had an opportunity to speak to other merchants in the village, she was forced to temper her anger. *Everyone* had received the same letter. Maybe Paul's motive was selfish, but at least his generosity extended to all the shopkeepers. If nothing else, Kathy had to be grateful for that, she decided with reluctance, especially when everyone was so happy.

Mrs. Armbruster, in particular, was overjoyed. "My dear, I've been positively despondent over the whole matter. When you get to be my age, you don't have a lot left in your life to give you purpose and joy. My tearoom gives me both."

Even though she had quite a way to go before she reached Mrs. Armbruster's age, Kathy agreed with everything the woman said.

Everyone needed joy and purpose in life. Her shop had given Kathy a purpose, and Paul had given her abundant joy. There was a chance she could lose her shop. Paul was already gone from her life. The letter gave her a reprieve for her business, but not for her heart.

—

When Kathy heard the door open and close, she looked up from her account books. "Marissa!" As soon as the name escaped from her, she regretted it. It seemed awfully informal and perhaps even rude for her to call such an elegant and polished woman, whom she had met once and then only in passing, by her first name. Marissa's mere presence among the yarns and paints of the shop seemed to elevate it to a level of chic Kathy wouldn't have thought possible.

At the sound of her name, Marissa advanced toward her with a warm smile. "Why, Kathy, how nice to see you again!" She glanced around the shop with considerable interest. "I had no idea you worked here. This is charming."

"Thank you." Swathed from neck to knee in a

royal purple cashmere sweater dress, Marissa was every bit as beautiful as Kathy remembered her. Kathy felt dowdy next to her. "The shop is mine," she added.

"Really? Well, that's wonderful! I was just telling CeCe"—she looked behind her, then turned fully around, the slightest of frowns marring her smooth brow—"CeCe?"

"I'm over here," came a disembodied voice. "I've just found the cutest little bears. No wonder you wanted to come in here!"

"CeCe and I just happened to be driving by and decided to stop in," Marissa explained. "You know, I'd forgotten that this little village was even here."

"A lot of people have," Kathy said ruefully. "Was there something in particular you were interested in?"

"Uh, no . . . not really. That is, I thought we could just look around, if that's all right."

"Of course."

"Marissa! You've just got to come see these bears! I'm going to buy the whole set!"

Kathy knew exactly what the unseen CeCe was talking about. On a table by the front window, she had set up a Christmas scene of a family of bears out taking a walk in the snow. She'd covered the table in bits of artificial snow and constructed a little town out of some of her ceramic village pieces. She followed Marissa behind the row of Christmas wreaths and ornament kits.

CeCe turned out to be a young woman about Kathy's own age who, just like Marissa, had an unmistakably sophisticated look about her. Blond and very attractive, CeCe smiled, and her blue eyes sparkled with delight. "Look, Marissa. Here are the papa and mama bears, and these two are their children. This whole thing is going to look just great on the table in my entryway."

Kathy cleared her throat. "I'm sorry. But that's for display. It's not for sale."

CeCe's mouth dropped briefly open before she let out something like a wail. "You can't mean it!"

Kathy nodded reluctantly. "You see, this is just an example of the things my customers can create with items from my store."

CeCe stared at her blankly. "I don't understand."

"You're supposed to make it yourself," Marissa said.

"*Make it!* Can't I just order one?"

CeCe had a most bewildered look on her face, and Kathy wondered how anyone so obviously spoiled could elicit her deepest sympathy. Nevertheless, she felt compelled to reassure the woman. "It's very easy. I sell everything right here in the shop to make the scene—the little village pieces, the houses, the church, the trees, even the street lamps. And of course, I have bears of all sizes. All you have to do is take bits of fabric, flowers, and ribbons, and hot-glue them onto the bears."

"I've never heard of heating glue before, have you, Marissa?"

"No, I can't say that I have."

Kathy smiled. "I have an area set up where I can demonstrate. It seems to be a bit slow in the store now, so if you like, I can show you how to make the mama bear. Then you can take the supplies home and do the other bears yourself."

CeCe grabbed Marissa's hand. "We have time, don't we? I'd love to try it."

**Get one full-length Loveswept FREE every month!**
Now you can be sure you'll never, ever miss a single Loveswept title by enrolling in our special reader's home delivery service. A service that will bring you all six new Loveswept romances each month for the price of five—and deliver them to you before they appear in the bookstores!

**Examine 6 Loveswept Novels for**

# 15 days FREE!

(SEE OTHER SIDE FOR DETAILS)

BUSINESS REPLY MAIL

FIRST-CLASS MAIL PERMIT NO. 2456 HICKSVILLE, NY

Postage will be paid by addressee

Loveswept
Bantam Books
P.O. Box 985
Hicksville, NY 11802

NO POSTAGE
NECESSARY
IF MAILED
IN THE
UNITED STATES

"Sure. I think it would be fun."

Kathy led the two ladies to her "project corner." She seated CeCe in one of the chairs, plugged in the glue gun, and collected all the materials that were needed to make the mama bear.

Once that was done, she set about explaining the project to CeCe while Marissa watched.

"See, we have a strip of six-inch lace in this pretty dusty rose color for the skirt. You simply thread this tapestry needle with this narrow ribbon and run it through the top of the lace. Then draw the lace together to make the gathered skirt and hot-glue the skirt onto her. Later, you can add a sash of half-inch ribbon around the waist to give it a finished look. We have two pieces of lace to make her top, and there's this dainty pearl necklace to go around her neck. For her head,"—Kathy picked up a cellophane package of pink satin roses—"I'll show you how to make a coronet out of these by twining narrow pink and white ribbon through them. Streamers will fall down her back from the coronet."

"This is great! What do I do first?"

The look of enthusiasm on CeCe's face did Kathy's heart good. If she could somehow attract a hundred more women like CeCe, maybe her shop would have a chance of surviving.

Kathy picked up two pieces of dusty rose lace that she had already cut. "You hot-glue these onto her, diaper fashion, front first, then back, for her panties."

"Oh, Marissa, isn't that cute?"

Marissa nodded. "Darling."

As far as Kathy could tell, Marissa seemed absolutely serious. But Kathy found it hard to believe that someone like the perfectly put-together Marissa, who had obviously never had to lift a finger in her life, could possibly enjoy watching an arts-and-crafts lesson. She had no further time to ponder the situation, though, because just then another customer walked in.

"I can't believe it, three customers at once," she muttered before she'd realized she'd said it aloud. "CeCe, you go ahead and do just as I told you. Just remember to hold each piece of lace in place for about ninety seconds, so that it seals."

The last thing she saw before she turned away to help the new customer was CeCe reaching for the glue gun. But two minutes later, a loud wail brought her attention back to the project area. "Excuse me a moment. I'll be right back," she murmured to the expensively dressed matron who seemed inordinately interested in the needlework kits, even though she didn't seem to know how to do them.

As soon as she reached the table, she saw what was wrong. CeCe had hot-glued three of her long, sculptured, acrylic fingernails to a piece of lace. "Oh, my," was all Kathy could think to say.

Marissa broke out laughing.

"What am I going to do?" CeCe asked. Her perfectly made-up face crinkled anxiously.

'I think I'd better get you to your manicurist immediately," Marissa managed to say before she went off into another peal of laughter. "She's going to have to replace those three nails."

"That's not necessary," Kathy quickly added, visions dancing in her head of a paying customer escaping. "Just run hot water over it for a while and the glue will peel right off."

"No, I think Marissa's right," CeCe said, getting up and walking quickly toward the front door, the lace dangling from her three nails. Kathy found herself faintly surprised that CeCe hadn't demanded that she call the paramedics. Amazingly, though, CeCe paused before she disappeared out the door. "Save all my stuff. I'll be back tomorrow to finish it."

"Bye, Kathy," Marissa called with a smile. "We'll see you tomorrow."

Strongly doubting that she'd ever see either woman again, Kathy went back to her other customer, who, amazingly enough, had chosen five needlepoint kits to purchase.

That night she suffered through a spell of loneliness. Nonetheless, she ate a good supper and turned in early. The next few days seemed to fly by. Every once in a while, though, she found herself gazing out the window, longing for a glimpse of a long, chocolate brown limousine or a dark green Jaguar. Then she realized what she was doing and abruptly got back to work.

Marissa and CeCe did indeed return, and CeCe was able to finish the mama bear without further incident, even though the coronet was glued on slightly askew. CeCe was so delighted with herself that she bought all the materials to make the whole scene. Kathy nearly burst into song as she rang up the sizable sale.

CeCe came back a day later to ask Kathy if she would take on the job of decorating her whole house for Christmas. "I have a passel of nieces and nephews coming in for the holidays, and I thought it would be fun to use teddy bears throughout. But I could never begin to do it all myself."

Kathy was immediately interested. "The teddy bears will be adorable, and we can also make toy soldiers and drums and perhaps use a few antique toys. And we could have ropes of garland with lights and colorful, long curling ribbons draping the rooms and staircase."

CeCe beamed. "I knew you'd come up with something! I can't wait to begin. This will be fun. And I bet that a lot of my friends will want you to do their homes, too."

"I'm not a decorator."

"No, but you know how to put things together in a fresh way."

Kathy could only say a prayer of thanks. Her expectations were being fulfilled. Christmas did seem to be bringing in more customers. Quite a few well-dressed ladies drifted into the shop, and they seemed genuinely intrigued at the idea of making their own centerpieces. Word of mouth was at work. Friends were bringing friends.

And it wasn't just Kathy's shop that was profiting. One or two of the ladies had brought in an armload of designer dresses to Judith's gently used clothing store. Judith reported that the two ladies had been really excited about the idea of cleaning out their extensive closets.

Kathy watched all the activity with fingers crossed, hoping that the busy streak would last.

Kathy smiled as she counted the money from the shop's cash register. It was dark outside now, but it had been a wonderful day. A cold front had even come in the night before, dropping temperatures into the forties. The weatherman had reported that there was an even colder front behind this one. Now all they needed was some precipitation—snow! Things were definitely looking up!

And she didn't care about the fact that she hadn't heard from Paul. Or so she told herself. Constantly.

Just then a young man of about nineteen walked in. Kathy opened her mouth to tell him the store was closed, but then thought better of it. Since when did she turn away a customer?

"May I help you?"

His dark eyes darted toward the door, then back to her, and he gave her a charming, lopsided grin. "Yeah, you can." He reached into his jacket pocket and pulled out a knife. With a push of a button, a long blade flicked from its hiding place, lethal and shining. "You can give me all the money you've got in that register."

She stared at him dumbly. The charming grin disappeared, and now she noticed that his eyes were dilated and glassy.

"Lady, the money!"

"But I don't have very much!"

The muscles in his neck were corded and strained as he advanced toward her and rounded the counter. "Whatever it is, I *want* it."

"But—" All she could think of was how desperately she needed the money, and how this person was going to take it away from her.

With a sudden move, he held the knife under her chin. "Now. Very carefully. Open the drawer."

How did such a young man get to be so menacing? she wondered, but realized that now wasn't exactly the time for sociological questions. Keeping her head as level as possible, she reached to her right and punched a key on the register. The drawer sprang open.

"Now that's a pretty lady," the young man crooned. "Take out all the money and put it on the counter." When she did, he grabbed the green bills and stuffed them in his pockets. "Show me where your safe is."

"I—I don't have a safe."

The knife pricked at her skin, drawing blood. Kathy's stomach rolled with nausea and fear.

"Don't lie to me, pretty lady. Every store has a safe."

*"Except this one."*

*Paul!* If the knife hadn't been digging into the soft flesh beneath her chin, Kathy would have sagged with relief at the sound of his voice.

The young man jerked Kathy in front of him and brought the knife around to the middle of her back. He eyed Paul cautiously. "Don't try to be a hero, man."

"Please don't hurt her."

A grin spread across the young man's face. "She's gonna go out of here with me. Whether she's hurt or not depends on you. Just get out of the way!"

Paul took a step to the side. The robber began to back away, dragging Kathy around the counter. Her heart was pounding so hard she could barely hear anything. She could see Paul's eyes and, in them, the mirrored image of her fear. She had to keep her head and stay on her toes, she told herself.

Once around the counter, the robber moved faster, but he was watching Paul so intently, his feet became tangled in some ornamental baskets stacked on the floor. He stumbled. As he tried to regain his balance, his grip loosened, giving Kathy just the opportunity she needed.

She tore out of his arms, and at the same time, Paul lunged for him. The two men struggled. Paul was stronger, but the young man had desperation on his side. He raised his arm and thrust. The knife sliced through Paul's sweater and plunged into the flesh of his right shoulder.

"Paul!" Kathy's scream was filled with horror.

Pain exploded in Paul's shoulder, but he grabbed the robber's wrist and pushed. The bloody knife came out and hovered in the air between the two men as they struggled for control.

Stricken with terror, Kathy whirled around and reached for the first heavy object she saw—a brass container filled with a Christmas arrangement. Using all the strength she could muster, she brought it down on the back of the man's head with a thud. He fell back, collapsing onto the hardwood floor.

Clutching his shoulder, Paul kicked the knife away from the inert body on the floor, then walked over to pick it up.

"Paul, are you all right?"

"Yes. Call the police."

Kathy knew a moment of indecision. Her first and strongest instinct was to rush to Paul. His face had lost all color, and blood marked the shoulder of his crewneck sweater, creating a spreading, red stain over the white cable knit. "I need to get something to use as a pressure bandage," she murmured, glancing around, feeling almost as much in shock as the injured Paul.

"Call the police!" Teeth gritted against the pain, Paul leaned back against a shelf for support. At his feet, the young man who had stabbed him opened his eyes and stared dazedly.

Kathy rushed to the phone and dialed 911. Within two minutes the police had arrived, and shortly thereafter, the paramedics.

At the hospital, Kathy held Paul's hand while the doctor treated and bandaged his wound. She had no idea if her presence was a comfort to him. All she knew was she couldn't bear for him to be out of her sight.

"You'll need to stay here at least overnight, maybe a little longer," the doctor was saying as he pressed the last piece of tape into place over the thick, gauze padding.

"No."

Paul's comment elicited no surprise from the doctor. Kathy realized that the physician probably encountered quite a few arguments from stubborn patients.

"Mr. Garth, it's for your own good. We need to keep you under observation. Your wound was very deep. Fortunately, no bone or artery was hit, but from this point on, any number of complications could develop."

"I'm not spending one night in this hospital." Paul stared at Kathy. "It's all white."

That statement *did* appear to surprise the doctor. "I beg your pardon?"

"Never mind." A spasm of pain crossed Paul's face as he struggled to sit up. "I'm going home."

The overworked doctor let out a weary sigh. "I can't stop you, but I hope at least you'll have someone there to look after you."

Paul paused, then cast a strange look at Kathy. "I live alone in a hotel. Can I have my shirt, Kathy?"

At Paul's request, Kathy called Robert. The chauffeur had picked up a clean shirt and a butter-soft suede jacket for Paul, then met them at the hospital. Kathy held the shirt out for Paul, and he gingerly slipped his arms into it.

The doctor scribbled on Paul's chart. "Well, then, going home is out of the question. A hotel room is no place for someone with an injury like yours. You're going to be in a great deal of pain."

Paul remained silent, deciding not to mention that his "hotel room" was a nine-room suite at the top of one of Dallas's most luxurious hotels, or that Robert lived in a suite on the same floor.

Kathy spoke up. "The doctor's right, Paul. You can't go back to a hotel."

"Then I'll go home with you."

"What?"

"You'll take care of me, won't you?"

"Well—"

Paul gave her no time to reply. "Then it's all set. Doctor, just tell us what to do."

# Six

Kathy could never have refused Paul's wish to stay at her place. In truth she would do anything to help him. She realized that Paul could have been killed, and the thought haunted her. She didn't know what had brought him to her store at the moment of the robbery, but he'd been injured while trying to protect her and her property. Honor decreed that she care for him. Honor—and her love for him.

Robert helped Kathy get Paul settled as comfortably as possible into her bed. Then he went out to get the antibiotic and painkiller the doctor had prescribed for Paul. By the time the chauffeur left again, Paul was wearing black silk pajama bottoms and had been given his first dose of medication.

Although he said very little about his discomfort, Kathy could tell he was in a great deal of pain.

"That painkiller isn't doing any good, is it?"

A ghost of a smile appeared. "It's hard to tell."

Kathy hovered over him. "What can I do for you?"

"Sit and talk to me."

"Okay." She dragged a straight-back chair over to the bed.

"Not there. Here." With his left hand, Paul pointed to a place beside him on the bed.

He was resting back against a pile of pillows. Light from the bedside lamp played over the width of his naked chest, covered with thick brown hair. There was a large bandage over his right shoulder, and his arm was in a navy blue sling.

Still, she hesitated. "I'm afraid I'll hurt you."

"It will only hurt if I have to twist around to see you."

It made sense. She sat down beside him, taking great care not to jar the bed.

He brought his hand down to her knee. "How are you? You don't look so good. Why wouldn't you let the doctor examine you?"

"Because you were the one who was hurt. Not me." She lifted her chin and touched the knife wound. "It stopped bleeding almost immediately."

For a moment he shut his eyes, a grim expression coming over his face. "When I saw him holding that knife to your throat, I was ready to kill him."

"Instead, he almost killed you. A few inches lower and that knife would have gone through your heart."

His hand tightened over her knee. "But it didn't. Thank you for letting me stay here."

The light laugh she gave revealed the mixed feelings she had regarding him staying in her apartment. "I don't have much room here . . . and I don't know what we're going to do about tomorrow. I'll have to be at the shop, you know."

"Robert will look in on me."

"And he couldn't have at the hotel?"

He shut his eyes again. "No."

She watched him for a moment. The pallid tone of his skin in no way diminished the strong line of his jaw, but he looked tired. She glanced at her watch, surprised to see that it was only nine o'clock. After all that had happened, it seemed much later. "Paul?" She spoke softly. "You should eat something. How about some soup? I'm sure with all the stuff you bought the other day—"

"Maybe in a little while."

She waited until he fell into a light sleep, then got up and went into the other room. Later, she made a bed for herself on the couch, but Paul's restlessness gave her little chance for sleep. Around midnight, she held his head while he drank a cup of beef broth, then she gave him another pain pill.

Just as before, she waited until he fell asleep before getting up. She was at the door when she heard him say, "Where are you going?"

She glanced over her shoulder to see him looking at her with sleepy eyes. "I've made a bed on the couch."

"Stay here with me."

She resented the way her pulses jumped at his request. "I don't think that's a very good idea. I might move the wrong way in the night and hurt you."

He pulled back the covers on the side of the bed opposite his wound. "I'd rather hurt with you than without you."

The debate she held with herself was short, and in the end she was glad she had given in, because he did seem to rest better with her beside him. Eventually she was also able to sleep.

Robert arrived early the next morning, and Paul insisted that the chauffeur drive her to work. She didn't think it was worth getting into an argument, with Paul being as weak as he was, so she agreed. That night, Robert also picked her up, and when she got home, she found that a phone had been installed.

"I had to have it," Paul explained from his position on the bed. "Business."

"You mean you've been conducting business today?"

"Not much," he admitted.

He appeared exhausted. His lids were half closed so that his eyelashes formed shadows on his pale cheeks, and his words were terse, as if the day had consumed all his energies.

She sat down beside him and took his hand. "What did the doctor say today when Robert took you to see him?"

"So far so good. Come back tomorrow."

"Did he suggest that you should be in the hospital?"

"No." His lids dropped over his eyes, but he lightly squeezed her hand. "Stop worrying."

"I can't help it. You wouldn't be in this predicament if it wasn't for me."

Her remark drew a smile from him, but he remained silent.

"Are you hungry? I'll fix you something."

"I'm not hungry now. Beth Ann dropped by earlier and made me eat something."

"Oh."

He squeezed her hand again. "Go eat dinner. There's some beef stew for you. All you have to do is heat it up."

"Beef stew?"

"Beth Ann cooked it up. Swears it cures all ills. Even stab wounds. It's from an old family recipe."

"I have an old family recipe called Connecticut Tea," she said before she thought. The sight of Paul looking so pale and helpless was terribly unsettling to her. She wanted to take away his pain and make him feel better, but since she couldn't do that, she wanted to do something constructive. She wanted to nurture him.

"Is it anything like iced coffee?" he asked.

"Not exactly. But I can guarantee it will cure just about anything. The problem is, I don't think it's all that nutritious, and it has a way of sometimes creating new problems. We'd better stick with Beth Ann's stew for now."

"Maybe you can make it for me tomorrow."

She rose from the bed and stood for a moment, watching his breathing become more even and peaceful as he fell asleep. "Maybe I will when you're better," she said softly, knowing she never would. Because as soon as he recovered, he'd be leaving her life and going back to his own.

She slept beside him again that night, aware of his every movement. The farther away she was from him, the more he tended to move about. The closer she was to him, the quieter he became.

The next night when she came home from work, there was a large, portable, color television at the foot of the bed.

"What's this for?"

Paul smiled to himself at the suspicious tone of her voice, aware that if she thought he'd bought it for her, she'd never accept it. "It's a big box with pretty colored pictures inside it that move and make noise."

Her eyes narrowed on him. "You must be feeling better."

"A little. I slept on and off today. The visit to the doctor wore me out, though. By the way, they changed the bandage and said everything looks fine."

"How's the pain?"

He made a face. "It's still there. I'll have another pain pill in an hour or so."

"Take it now if you're hurting."

He shook his head and smiled wearily. "Those pills make me feel like my head's filled with cotton. I want to be alert for at least a little while this evening."

She walked to the bed, bent over him, and laid her hand on his forehead. She was relieved to find his skin cool. "That's silly. Quit trying to be brave."

"Who? Me?" He laughed, then groaned at the pain. "I may be cured forever of being brave."

"I hope so," she said fervently. "You might have been killed."

"You, too."

She straightened and stared down at him, disconcerted at the hint of concern in his voice. Although she was glad he was here in her apartment, his presence was a constant reminder of what couldn't be.

"A new security patrol started today at the village," she said.

"Good."

"I suppose that was your doing?"

He nodded. His expression told her that if she wanted to argue the matter, she would get nowhere. Besides, she thought, she couldn't really object to something that benefited the other eleven tenants of the village.

Her eyes lit on the expensive television, something she *could* object to. "About this set—"

"It's for me. Okay? I get bored just lying here in bed all day. I like to watch football games. The news. Stock market quotations."

Kathy rubbed her forehead. She supposed it would be tedious having to lie in bed all day long, especially for an active man like Paul.

"Weather," he added.

Her interest quickened. "Weather? Really?" While working her way through college, she'd never had time to watch television. And since she'd been in Dallas, she hadn't been able to afford a set. "I forgot they gave weather reports on television. When do they come on?"

"Six and ten o'clock."

She checked her watch. "Shoot! It's seven. Right in between."

He chuckled and ignored the surge of pain. "Beth Ann had the chef of one of my favorite restaurants make up an order of beef Stroganoff for us. Everything's waiting in the oven."

She tore her gaze away from the television. "What? Oh, no! That oven will have dried everything out by now. It's old and cantankerous."

Paul felt his strength ebbing, but he managed to hold up his left hand. "Everything's fine. Robert brought in a warming oven."

"A portable warming oven?" Now she'd heard of everything.

He lay back against the pillows and shut his eyes. "Bring a tray in here, and we'll eat together. Then I'll take the pain pill."

Later that evening, Paul was nearly asleep when he heard Kathy beside him give an excited squeal. Without opening his eyes, he asked, "What?"

"The weatherman says we may have snow in three days. Isn't that great?"

"If you say so."

"Tell Skye not to worry about me, James," Paul said into the receiver. "I'm getting stronger every day."

"That's good," the deep voice of Paul's longtime friend and employer, James Steele, returned. "When we heard, we had the jet fueled up."

"No need to fly in. I'm getting very good care."

"I know. I checked."

Paul smiled. "And when James Steele checks

up on something, grown men tremble. I wondered why the doctor was extra gentle with me today."

"You're exaggerating."

"Hardly."

"How long do you think you'll be staying with Kathy?"

"For as long as I can. I sure didn't plan to get stabbed, but it couldn't have happened at a better time. Kathy had drawn away from me, and I wasn't sure how I was going to reach her. I'm hoping that this time together will help us."

James chuckled. "Underhanded methods. I approve."

With a smile, Paul settled more comfortably into the pillows. "I thought you'd understand the tactics involved, especially since you're more or less my role model."

"You're talking about how I kidnapped Skye to California, aren't you? Well, in our particular case, it worked. Each day of the past eight years has been better than the last. We have a blessed marriage. You'll have the same good fortune, one of these days."

Paul grimaced as a pain shot through his shoulder. He lifted his right elbow and shifted it to a more comfortable position in the sling. "This situation is a little different, James. You were in love with Skye from the first moment you laid eyes on her in the airport."

"Don't try to tell me you're not in love with Kathy. When you described her to Skye and me during your last visit, we assumed that at long last—"

Paul frowned. "Sarah—"

"Has been dead now for five years, and so should your guilt."

No one but James Steele would have dared talk to Paul in such a way. Because James was his friend, Paul took it. "Sarah was my wife, and although I haven't the slightest idea why, she loved me."

"Past tense. Let's speak present tense. What is Kathy?"

"The woman I want."

There was only silence on the other end of the line. When James spoke again, there was a change in his voice that Paul couldn't quite define.

"I've never known you to play anything but fair with a woman before, Paul. Kathy must really be something. Skye and I are dying to meet her."

"I'm sure you will, sooner or later."

"Look at that!" Kathy pointed with disgust at the weather map currently being shown on the television screen. "Can you believe it? The snow went north of us, up into Oklahoma!"

"I'm sorry."

The laughter in his voice made her look at him. Gratefully, she noticed that his color had improved over the past couple of days. Every once in a while she was even able to catch a twinkle in his eyes. Like now. "But the Panhandle and part of West Texas got snow!"

"That's just the way things work around here, and you should be glad. If we'd gotten snow, Dallas would have ground to a halt, and you would have had zero customers in your shop today."

"Maybe that wouldn't have happened. Maybe the snow would have given everyone the Christmas spirit, and I would have had more customers. It works for me."

"It doesn't work here in Dallas." A smile played around his mouth as he watched her. She was wearing jeans and a T-shirt with *Elvis* written in script across its front, and she was curled up on the end of the bed like a kitten. She no longer seemed selfconscious about sharing her bed with Paul, and that was good. He wanted her to be comfortable with him around. Then, after he recovered, perhaps she wouldn't ask him to leave.

His conversation with James had bothered him somewhat. James had assumed that he was in love with Kathy. Paul closed his eyes. *Love.* A woman like Kathy would be easy for any man to love. He was the problem. Paul Garth couldn't love any woman. His reasons were entangled in shadows and memories that haunted hard-to-reach places in his brain, but he had long ago accepted his limitations.

It didn't change the fact, though, that he was doing everything in his power to make sure that he and Kathy stayed together. If he couldn't love her, he could take care of her and make sure that she never wanted for anything again. They could make each other happy, he was convinced. He'd never been able to figure out why there was so much emphasis put on the emotion of love, anyway.

His eyes slowly opened to see that Kathy's attention was on the weather report. The weatherman announced that the next few days would be clear and sunny.

"Maybe if I try another channel." She picked up the remote control and pushed a different button.

"I've never known anyone so obsessed with the weather."

"I'm not obsessed. It's just that I'm used to Jack Frost nipping at my nose, and it's just not happening!"

This time he laughed aloud. "Don't worry. It's early yet. Sometimes we get a couple of inches in January."

"January! But that'll be too late! We need snow for Christmas!"

He lightly rubbed his right arm in an unconscious effort to ease the ache there. *Christmas.* It seemed to come earlier every year.

"How's Paul today?" Marissa asked as Kathy finished ringing up another customer's sale. "I talked to him yesterday, and he told me he was feeling better."

Kathy smiled at Marissa, happy to see her. "He seems to be on the mend. His recovery is slow, though."

"I think that's to be expected, isn't it? Paul told me that the wound was deep."

"It was. The doctor's been checking it every day."

"That's good." Marissa gave a delicate shudder. "It's so hard to believe that something like that could happen."

Kathy nodded in agreement. She wondered if she'd ever be able to erase from her mind the horrid memory of that knife sinking into Paul's shoulder.

With a sympathetic gesture, Marissa reached out and touched Kathy's arm. "It must have been awful for you. How are you doing?"

Kathy blinked. She'd been so worried about Paul over the past few days, she hadn't even thought about herself. "I'm fine. I wasn't hurt at all."

"I'm so glad." Marissa glanced around the shop.

"Is there something I can help you with?" Kathy asked. Marissa had been in the shop several times, but she'd always been accompanying someone else, and she had never bought anything.

"I want to make a wreath to go over my mantel."

"You want to *make* a wreath?"

Marissa's eyes sparkled with humor. "I can't let CeCe get the better of me, now can I? Besides, I'm having a little tree-decorating party at the end of next week, and I want something really special. Normally, I would have just ordered one from the decorators, but your enthusiasm for crafts is contagious, and I want to try my hand at creating one myself."

Kathy tried not to look too astounded. "Did you have something particular in mind?"

Marissa's gaze went to the wall where Kathy had hung the grapevine wreaths. "I'm going to need a big wreath, at least thirty-six inches," she murmured, ambling down the aisle.

Kathy followed. Although she knew very little about Marissa, she could tell that the beautiful, self-possessed woman would have very definite ideas.

The first thing Marissa did was select a wreath

and spray it gold. While it dried, she and Kathy roamed over the shop, choosing an astounding variety of things—fine gold netting, four kinds of ribbon, several sizes of translucent, iridescent ornaments, glittering, tinsel chenille stems, strings of glowing pearls, and a spray of delicate, gold-beaded filaments.

Most of the selections were Marissa's choice; Kathy merely showed her where things were. But by the time Kathy settled Marissa in her "project corner," she was caught up with the fantasy of the project. Fortunately, business was fairly good, but between customers Kathy checked on Marissa's progress.

"This is going to be just gorgeous," Kathy said, staring at the wreath sometime later.

Marissa sat back with a sigh of satisfaction. "Thanks. And listen, remember that little tree-decorating party I mentioned? I forgot to say that, naturally, you and Paul are invited."

"Oh, I don't know. Paul—"

"I know what you mean." Marissa reached for a spool of ribbon and began to form a bow on her fingers, looping and twisting, just as Kathy had showed her. "I hesitated over the invitation, but I've given the matter a lot of thought and decided it would be good for Paul. Too much time has passed for him to continue on like this."

Kathy wondered about Marissa's concept of time. It hadn't been that long at all since he'd been stabbed. "I suppose it would be all right, that is if he's feeling well enough and the doctor gives his okay."

Marissa gave her a surprised look. "Doctor?"

"He's not that strong yet, you know."

"Oh . . . No, I suppose not." She returned her attention to the bow.

There was something in Marissa's tone of voice that bothered Kathy. "We are talking about the same thing, aren't we? His health. The reason why you were hesitant to invite Paul to your party?"

The ribbon began uncurling from Marissa's fingers. She made a grab for it, hit the ribbon spool, and sent it spinning off the table and onto the floor where it rolled for a few feet, unraveling ribbon in its wake.

"Oops!" Marissa's husky laugh peeled out through the shop. "Sorry about that. It's going to take awhile to get the hang of this."

"Marissa—"

"Excuse me, miss?" A newcomer in the shop called for Kathy.

With a frustrated glance at Marissa, she went to help the customer.

By the time Kathy returned to the "project corner," Marissa was just putting the last item on the wreath—an ethereal angel, wearing a gold lamé gown with a silver shawl draped around her shoulders and over her arms.

Kathy sat down across from Marissa. "Look, there's something I don't understand. Why do you think it would be good for Paul to come to your party? And what did you mean about his continuing on like this?"

Marissa briefly met Kathy's gaze, then returned her attention to the wreath. "I really like you, Kathy. You're one of the nicest, loveliest people I've met in a long time. I couldn't be happier that you and Paul are together. But Paul has been my friend for a long time, and I would never want to betray a confidence. I shouldn't have said anything, but I assumed . . . Please, I'd just prefer that we drop the whole subject."

"Of course." Kathy studied Marissa's bent head, wondering why she felt such curiosity. After all, she already knew that things couldn't work out between her and Paul. He didn't love her, he just wanted her. He was only staying in her apartment because he had been wounded. When he was well enough and her novelty value for him had worn off, he'd go back to his own life. Still . . . "I understand why you wouldn't want to discuss Paul, but perhaps you could tell me a little about Sarah."

"Sarah?"

"It's just that Paul never talks about her."

"That's natural, don't you think?" Marissa's tone was careful. "It's been five years since her death."

"I guess so. But he must have loved her very much not to have remarried after all this time."

Marissa sat back with a sigh and regarded Kathy solemnly. "Sarah was my best friend, but I don't think it's biased of me to say that everyone adored her. She was absolutely wonderful. Her death affected Paul a great deal, as it did all of us."

"Of course." Kathy suddenly felt ashamed, probing into an obviously painful area.

"It's finished."

"Finished?"

"The wreath. It's finished."

The wreath took Kathy's breath away. It was a vision of gossamer gold netting, glittering bits of sparkle, iridescent glass, and ropes of pearls. "It's fantastic."

Marissa nodded in agreement, her solemn mood apparently gone now. "I can't wait to see it over my fireplace. And you'll be able to see for yourself how it looks the night of the party. You will come, won't you?"

Kathy hedged. "If Paul feels up to it."

An elegant hand waved in dismissal. "Paul will come if I have to hire an ambulance to bring him."

"Really? Well, there's just one more thing."

"What's that?"

She still didn't have a decent wardrobe. "What will everyone be wearing?"

"Oh, come casual. We get more than enough formal affairs this time of year."

Kathy swallowed and managed a smile.

# Seven

"Why don't you fix us something to snack on during the football game?" Paul suggested.

"Like what?" She was not really surprised that he was only asking her to fix a snack. There'd been an overabundance of food in her apartment since Paul had come to stay, but somehow she never had to cook any of it. There seemed to be an endless number of restaurants in the Dallas area eager to send over meals for Paul Garth. By the time she got home from work each evening, a mouth-watering dinner was waiting in the warming oven. She was sure she'd gained at least ten pounds. Some days it felt like fifteen.

His friends also brought food to him. She never met any of these friends, but she knew that they visited because she found new dishes of food every evening. Sometimes she wondered what his fancy friends must think about the idea of Paul recuperating in the small garage apartment of a girl they'd never met. But she usually didn't have time to worry about it.

More and more people were discovering Bluebonnet Village, bolstering business in all the shops, and keeping her and the other shop owners busy. To Kathy, it was like a miracle. And renovations had started, creating even more activity. The shop owners scrambled to adjust, but none of them grumbled.

"There's a flat white dish in the refrigerator that has some gluey orange stuff in it," Paul was saying. "It's a cheese dip. All you have to do is microwave it for a few minutes until it softens and heats."

The microwave was one of many new additions to her apartment. One day she'd come home and it had been sitting on its own little cart, all gleaming and efficient and ready for her to use. In fact, her kitchen now boasted so many new gadgets and appliances, there was no spare counter or floor space. All of it, Paul insisted, was vital to his recuperation. Kathy had given up arguing, figuring that when Paul left, so would all the state-of-the-art electronic and kitchen equipment.

"By the way, don't give any of the cheese dip to the mice," he said. "It's too spicy for them."

"*I'm* not the one who's feeding them these days. I've never seen two fatter, healthier mice in my life."

He gave her a guileless smile. "As you once told me, they've got to live, too."

"Uh-huh."

Ten minutes later, she was back in the bedroom, placing a tray at the foot of the bed.

"Great. You're just in time. They're about to kick off."

Kathy made no comment as she took her place beside him on the bed. She'd never had the time or the interest to follow sports, but on this particular Sunday afternoon, Paul had convinced her to watch this play-off game with him. Somehow she found it endearing that a sophisticated man like Paul could get so excited about a little ball being carried up and down a field of grass.

Crossing her jean-clad legs, she bent forward, grabbed the tray, and pulled it to her. "Are these the chips you wanted?" There was so much food in the kitchen, she wasn't always sure she was putting the right things together.

"Those are great." He reached out and patted her knee. "Thank you. I'm sorry for all the work I'm causing you."

"What work? I never do anything more than heat things up."

"Yes, but I've sort of taken over your apartment. I know my stay here's a big inconvenience."

There was a disturbing softness in his eyes as he looked at her. Today, the gray glints that had first intrigued her were very much in evidence. She looked away and down only to encounter the royal blue silk pajama bottoms he had on this afternoon. Moodily, she wondered if the store from which he bought his pajamas only sold *bottoms*. "After what you've been through, this was hardly an inconvenience."

He placed an unexpected kiss on her cheek. "I

want you to know that I appreciate it. You've made me feel very comfortable."

Unbidden, her hand flew to her cheek to touch the place where his lips had been. It was the first kiss he'd given her since the day she'd come to his office and discovered he was president of the Hayes Corporation. It meant nothing to her, she told herself. And she didn't want him to kiss her again, on the lips. Just as lying beside him in bed every night didn't make her ache with need. *Sure, Kathy.*

"The game's started," she said, her voice a weak imitation of itself.

He didn't say anything, but he gently gave her cheek a caress before he turned his attention to the game.

Kathy sank back against the pillows. Her eyes were on the television, but her mind was on the man beside her. He was a long way from being a hundred percent well again, but every day she could see improvement. He still didn't have use of his right arm, but every other part of his body worked beautifully. And so did hers.

The last few mornings she'd awakened earlier than he, to feel the warmth of his body, along with an unmistakable hardness, pressed against her. Heat had flared in her before she'd had a chance to check it, and she'd been forced to scurry to the bathroom for a cold shower.

"Which team are you rooting for?" she asked, desperate to change her train of thought.

"California, of course."

"That's right. You grew up in California. That's why you can drive."

He laughed, picked up her hand, and squeezed it. "You may not realize this, but learning to drive is sort of a constitutional right for most Americans—especially teenage boys! You just happen to be from one of the places that has mass transit."

She thought about it for a moment. "I suppose that's true. What part of California are you from?"

"Santa Barbara. My parents still live there, as do an assortment of aunts, uncles, and cousins."

"Really?"

He grinned. "You sound surprised that I have parents. I visit them every time I fly out there. *They* actually like me."

Now it was her turn to laugh. "You're making it sound as if I don't."

"Well, you do plan to kick me out as soon as I can manage on my own, don't you?"

His tone was teasing, but there was an underlying seriousness that made her squirm uncomfortably. "Don't you want to watch the game?" she asked.

"There's a commercial on."

"Oh. So where did you go to school?"

"UCLA and the Harvard Business School. And then I was lucky enough to hook up with James Steele."

"That was lucky," she acknowledged.

"He and his wife want to meet you."

*"What?"* She almost fell off the bed.

"It's only natural. They're two of my closest friends."

"But why would they want to meet me?"

"Oh, I don't know. I guess because I've told them a lot about you."

"Great." She sank back into the pillows, completely thrown by the thought that the larger-than-life James Steele had been told about her and wanted to meet her. "The game's back on."

"Do you think you could hand me my soda?"

"Oh, sure. Absolutely." She reached for the glass and handed it to him.

He took a few sips. "They're nice people, you know."

"Nice. Like you. Right?"

Paul glanced at her out of the corner of his eye, unsure why she was suddenly in such a bad mood. Taking a few sips of soda, he studied the television screen and noted that his team was whipping the opposing team. He decided not to point out that the team currently losing was from the Northeast.

He threw another glance at her. Her arms were crossed over her chest, and her face was set. He'd told her that two of his friends wanted to meet her and she'd become angry. After thinking about it, he decided he knew why. Before he was stabbed, she'd had every intention of ending their relationship. She still intended to do that as soon as he was recovered, so she was trying her best to keep a safe distance between them.

Sometimes he wondered if he was doing the wrong thing in being so singleminded in his determination to make sure that she would be his. Almost from the start, he'd manipulated every situation to his advantage. He regretted his relentless control, but given the choice of having her or not having her, he'd do the same things again.

Was he doing wrong? If he just stopped trying

and walked away, would she be happier? He wasn't sure. To him, *right* was having Kathy with him so he wouldn't have to worry about whether she was eating, or taking care of herself, or riding that damned bicycle in traffic. Maybe if he exited the scene, she'd have a chance to find a man who could give her the love she deserved. And yet, he couldn't let her go—not now, not ever.

"Kathy, would you mind scooping a chip into that cheese dip and feeding it to me?" He was holding his drink in his good hand.

The expression on her face told him she wasn't happy about the chore, but she bent forward, scooped up some cheese on a large chip, and brought it to his mouth.

He took it with one bite. As he did, he brushed his lips against her fingers and saw her wince as if he had burned her. He waited a few minutes. "Could I have another, please?"

She sent him a speaking glance, but did as he asked. This time, some of the cheese ran over on her fingers. Instead of biting the chip, he darted out his tongue to lick the errant cheese from her fingers.

He saw the green of her eyes darken and the hand that gripped the chip tremble. Holding her gaze, he parted his lips as if he were waiting for her to put the chip into his mouth. But they both knew he was waiting for something else.

She seemed paralyzed. She didn't move. She didn't breathe. She didn't blink. Then a tremor ran through her. After a moment she inserted the cheese-laden chip between his lips.

Keeping his eyes on her, he savored the spicy

flavor of the dip. When he swallowed, he saw her gaze go to the column of his throat and follow the motion. Behind them the television blared, and he heard the crowd cheer. He had no idea what was happening with the game, and he didn't care. He had only used the game as an excuse to get her to spend some waking time close beside him.

Again he parted his lips. He could have been silently asking for another chip, but he wasn't, and they both knew it. He saw Kathy take a shuddering breath. His mouth formed the word *please.*

Mesmerized, she swayed toward him. Then suddenly she jumped off the bed before he could stop her.

"I don't want to watch the game anymore!" she shouted and retreated to the other room, badly shaken.

Kathy spent the next two hours busying herself, sorting through some beads and ribbons that she'd brought home. But when she finished, the objects were still in the same muddled piles.

For once in her life, why couldn't something be easy for her? she asked herself. Why couldn't she simply tune Paul out so that he didn't affect her so much? Why did she have to be so overpoweringly aware of him?

Time dragged. She could hear the noise from the television, but Paul didn't call to her. Finally she walked back to the bedroom, afraid that he might need something. She found him asleep.

She stood beside the bed and gazed down at him worriedly. The pallor of his skin seemed more pronounced tonight. She studied him more closely and decided that maybe her imagination was working overtime. His breathing was even, and he seemed to be resting well.

When she checked on him fifteen minutes later, she found him awake. Trying to act as if nothing had happened between them, she scurried around the room, straightening things. "How are you feeling?"

"A little stiff. I've been lying here all afternoon. I need to get up and move around."

"That's probably a good idea. Would you like to have dinner at the kitchen table?"

He nodded and rubbed his chest. "That sounds good. First I'd like a bath, though. I'm feeling grubby."

"A bath? But hasn't Robert always helped you with your baths since you were injured?"

"Yes, but he's off this weekend. You'll have to do it."

*"Me!"*

"Kathy, I can't manage by myself. I can't move my right arm very well, and I have to keep the dressing dry."

He was making everything sound so reasonable, but she knew it wasn't. "You can make do, though, I'm sure."

"Maybe. Maybe not. I couldn't wash my back. My balance getting in and out of the tub would be iffy. Trying it would really tire me out." He smiled. "Kathy, what's the problem? You've seen me without clothes before, and you've even seen me in the tub."

Heat flared in her face. Without another word, she turned on her heels and went to draw his water.

• • •

The water was clear and hot and only reached to his navel, a precaution to keep his bandaged shoulder dry. He was reclining against the back of the tub, his left arm resting along the rim, his eyes closed.

Kneeling on the floor, Kathy gripped the washcloth with a hand that wasn't quite steady. "This shouldn't take long," she said, determinedly bright. "I've got our dinner warming."

"The warming oven won't dry it out."

"I used my regular oven."

The smile that crinkled the corners of his mouth made her suddenly feel transparent. She brought the cloth down on his chest with a scrubbing action that she had used many times on her kitchen floor.

His eyes flew open. "Ouch!"

"Sorry," She lessened the force, gentling the pressure. His chest seemed endlessly wide as she ran the washcloth across it, then back again. The dark hairs that covered his chest lathered up, becoming even softer than normal. She longed to toss the washcloth aside and use her hands, but she steeled herself against the desire. *Just wash him and get it over with, Kathy.*

The lapping of the water sounded unnaturally loud in the quiet of the bathroom, and the soap was scented with the spice-and-lime cologne he wore. It was a scent that could drug her, even captivate her.

She drew the cloth in a circle around one of his nipples, then over it. A moan came from his throat, but the sound was so faint that after a moment she decided she hadn't really heard it. She continued on to the other nipple, giving more attention to the job than she had intended.

She decided to move on to another part of his body, a safer part that wouldn't make her want to linger and caress. As she was debating exactly where this might be, he leaned forward, offering his back.

His back! Of course! What could be safer? But Paul's back was a smooth expanse of rippling muscles. Its potential strength fascinated her.

And as she leaned forward to reach down to his waist, her breast pressed against his arm, resting along the rim of the tub. It had been so long since he had touched her breasts; now the contact inflamed her.

All at once, it seemed as if the small bathroom was shrinking. She felt closed in, with no air to breathe, and a fire was burning deep inside her.

Abruptly she pulled away, and he leaned back in the tub, drawing up a leg as he did so. She looked at the leg. *Why not?* she thought.

Keeping her eyes determinedly off the area where his thighs met, she applied more soap to the washcloth, then skimmed it down the length of his leg. She encountered hard muscles that bewitched her. The least movement on his part made the muscles flex. And there was also a covering of dark hair on his legs that she could brush one way and then another, making patterns and paths. In a way it was like child's play, only it wasn't.

She couldn't look into his eyes, but instead concentrated on the washing. With each sweep of the cloth, she found herself bringing it higher up his thigh. The inside of his thigh was particularly fascinating. The muscles were no less hard there, but his skin seemed more pliable. Once, the cloth slipped out of her hand, and her palm came into contact with his skin. The water had made his skin warm, the soap had made it slick. Just for a moment she gave herself up to the luxury of feeling him, flesh against flesh.

"Kathy . . ." His voice was a husky whisper that touched every nerve-ending in her body.

She grabbed for the cloth. "I think you're clean."

"There's one place you haven't washed."

"Your face. I think you can wash that."

"I wasn't talking about my face."

Unerringly her eyes were drawn to his lap. His male sexuality stood rigid and proud. "I . . . don't think so."

His voice broke as he whispered, "Touch me, Kathy."

The washcloth fell from her nerveless fingers. "I . . ." She extended her hand, wanting to take hold of him, to feel the strength of him, the length of him. She tried to swallow, but couldn't. Her hand got closer and closer until she was so close, she could actually feel the heat that radiated from him.

"Kathy . . ." He reached for her, his hand sliding around the back of her neck.

She scrambled to her feet. "You'll have to finish by yourself," she mumbled and fled the room.

Kathy sat back on her heels and stared at the little Christmas tree she'd brought home that evening strapped to the handlebars of her bicycle. Over Paul's and, surprisingly, Robert's objections, she had resumed her pattern of pedaling herself to and from the shop.

It had been several days since the incident in the bathroom. From that night on, she'd slept on the couch. Paul had made no comment, but his eyes constantly followed her, as if he were pondering some weighty matter.

Kathy hated the barrier of tension between them. She realized that she was stiff with him, more reserved. But what else could she do? She couldn't allow a repeat of what had happened between them in the bathroom. Because if her guard ever dropped, if she went into his arms just once, she wouldn't have the strength to let him go.

She glanced over her shoulder and wasn't surprised to find him staring at her with the enigmatic gaze she'd learned to expect from him lately. He was lounging in a worn, comfortable chair in the living room.

"What do you think of the tree?" she asked, trying to gloss over the awkwardness she was feeling.

"I think it's the ugliest tree I've ever seen."

Her light red eyebrows rose in surprise. This was the first time Paul had ever uttered a harsh word to her. "Well, I know it's sort of a Charlie Brown tree. I mean, it's scraggly and sparse, and this limb here is longer than the others. But when I saw it in the tree lot, it seemed to be trying so hard to stand tall amongst all the other taller, fuller trees. Everyone was passing it by, making cruel jokes about it. My heart just went out to it. I had to buy this little tree, and it wasn't much money at all."

"Any money was too much."

Puzzled at his attitude and feeling a strange need to defend the tree, she turned around to face him. "It's going to be beautiful. I'm going to make origami ornaments for it. I brought home all the materials."

"Do what you want," he snapped. "You will, anyway, but personally I don't know why you bother."

She studied him for a moment. "Paul, are you in pain? You look strained. Maybe you should go lie down."

He rubbed his eyes with his thumb and forefinger. "I'm fine, and I'm sorry for being short with you. It's just that I'm not much of a Christmas person."

Kathy's brow wrinkled as she tried to understand. "Well, I guess a lot of folks aren't. There's so much to do and everything. They say depression is a big problem for some people this time of year."

His glance went to the little tree and back to her. "Obviously, you aren't one of those people."

"No. I've always loved Christmas. It's a magical time, a time of miracles and happiness and snow."

"When are you going to give up on snow?"

"Last night on the news, the weatherman was talking about a new front that's coming in from the north. I think it looks promising."

"Kathy, I hate to break this to you, but our worst weather—the rare bouts of snow and ice—always comes in from the southwest, swinging through El Paso, coming across the state, and picking up moisture from the gulf."

"Really? How odd."

He frowned at her flat tone. "Is snow so important to you? Are you that homesick?"

She turned back to the tree and fingered one of its thin branches. "Maybe my wanting snow is partly symptomatic of being homesick, but it's a very small part. I'd like to go back home and visit my friends and relatives, but I think that's natural. Even if I had the money, though, I wouldn't have the time. Business has really picked up. If things continue like this, I'll be able to afford that rent increase."

"Forget about the damned rent!"

She kept her back turned to him. The rent was one subject they would never agree on. And she was afraid snow was another.

"Kathy . . . tell me why snow is so important to you."

His voice had lost its harshness now and had taken on an imploring quality. Slowly she swiveled around to face him. "Why does one person love chocolate and another person love the color yellow? There isn't just one reason. I love to watch it fall. I love to walk in it. I love to fall down in it and make snow angels. I've never minded the inconvenience, and I've never spent a Christmas of my life without snow."

He had listened intently to her, his left elbow propped on the chair's arm, his chin resting in his palm. "There'll be no snow this year," he said quietly.

"Perhaps," she said just as softly, caught by

something she couldn't quite make out in the blue depths of his eyes.

For a time, there was silence in the room. Paul was the first to speak. "Marissa came by today."

"Oh?" She threw a glance around the small, shabbily furnished room, trying to imagine the elegant Marissa, clothed in one of her designer dresses, strolling through. She failed.

"Marissa said she had invited us to her party, and she wanted to follow up on it to make sure we'd be there."

Kathy looked down at her hands. "I didn't mention it because I didn't know whether she was just being nice or not." *And because the idea that you and I are a couple is completely erroneous.*

Paul chuckled. "Marissa is a decisive lady; she never does anything unless she wants to."

Kathy recalled that Paul had once said the same thing about himself. It was just added proof that she and Paul weren't two of a kind. He needed someone like Marissa.

"She said you wanted to go."

"She did?" Kathy supposed that in trying to be polite, she had given Marissa that impression.

"If you want to, we'll go."

"Marissa said she thought it would be good for you."

His face clouded. "Marissa evidently fancies herself something of a psychiatrist."

Kathy couldn't quite believe it. First she had felt it necessary to defend the little tree, and now she was about to defend Marissa. "I got the impression she fancies herself your friend."

"She is. But in this case she needs to back off."

"So then you don't want to attend the party?"

He stared broodingly at her. "When she told me you wanted to go, I accepted the invitation."

# Eight

The truth was that Kathy felt uncomfortable about attending a party at Marissa's. She was sure she would feel out of place. But because of her, Paul had agreed to something he didn't want to do. Deep inside, she was touched by his thoughtfulness.

Kathy knew that something was troubling Paul, something more than his stab wound and her refusal to sleep with him. She didn't know what the problem was, and she wasn't sure she wanted to. There was no point in her getting more involved with him. No future. No happiness. She knew that as well as she knew her own name. She just wished it wasn't necessary to keep reminding herself.

But she was committed to go to the party, and once again she set out to find something wonderful to wear for next to nothing. Marissa had told her to come casual, but Kathy was sure that

Marissa's idea of casual simply meant no ball gowns.

As Judith's "gently worn" establishment had had a dramatic increase in business, the quality of the clothes that were being brought in had gone up considerably.

Kathy found a soft wool dress in a pale lavender color that made her red hair appear vibrantly alive. The problem was, the dress was trimmed with enough ruffles and froufrous to make a battleship look festive. But Kathy had a feeling about the dress. And her decision swung in favor of the dress when Judith let her have it for a "next-to-nothing" price. Judith even threw in an elegant pair of shoes as part of the deal.

She took the dress home, and once she stripped off all the ruffles and froufrous, she discovered that her instincts had been right. The dress was well cut and well made, but it still needed a little something else.

At the shop, she selected satin ribbon in shades of pink, mauve, and soft fuchsia. Then, using a combination of weaving and macramé, she made a belt for the dress.

The night of the party, she rolled her hair with the electric curlers her mother had once given her for a Christmas present. She hadn't used the set in years and was a little astonished by the finished product. The result was a dramatic abundance of hair that fell down her back in a mass of waves and curls.

Next, she slipped on the lavender dress and secured the satin ribbon belt around her waist, knotting the ribbons at the back and letting the ends trail down to the hem.

Finally, the look on Paul's face told her that all her efforts had succeeded.

When Robert pulled the limousine into the circular driveway of Marissa's house, Kathy couldn't believe what she saw.

"This can't be one person's house! It's big enough for the entire population of a Third World country!"

Amused, Paul said, "I assure you, this is Marissa's house, and she lives in it all alone. She has a couple who, between the two of them, are her housekeeper, cook, and butler, but they live in their own little house somewhere on the grounds. I've never been quite sure where, it's so well hidden."

"Good grief."

If Kathy had thought the facade of the house was incredible, the interior left her gaping. The rooms were decorated in white, silver and gold, and resembled a winter fairyland. A twenty-foot tree stood in one corner of the main room, twinkling with hundreds and hundreds of tiny white lights.

Marissa met them at the door wearing soft white leather pants and a white mohair sweater decorated with leather inserts and threads of silver. "I'm so happy you're finally here! Kathy, you look gorgeous! All that hair is fabulous, and that dress is just wonderful."

"Thank you."

"And Paul." Marissa tucked her arm through his good one. "That sling makes you look positively intriguing."

His eyebrows shot up as if he were offended. "You mean I don't normally look intriguing?"

"Naturally, darling, what I meant was *more* intriguing. *More.*"

"I thought that was what you meant."

She laced her other arm through Kathy's and led them into the crowd of people. Soon they were surrounded. Kathy was surprised to find that many of the women had been in her shop, and so she'd already met them. Before she knew it, she was caught up in the festive party. Sometime later, when she had a moment to think about it, she was amazed to realize that she wasn't feeling at all ill at ease.

Someone played Christmas carols on a shiny white baby grand, accompanied by the ever-changing groups of people who clustered around.

Silver baskets filled with ornaments sat on the floor at the foot of the tree. Garvey, a short, round man with very little hair, was one of the people decorating the tree at the moment. With great care, he hung a delicate crystal snowflake, then stood back to admire his handiwork.

"Sweetie, I think you should have hung it on this branch here," his wife Loraine said, pointing out a higher branch. Loraine was a long, tall Texan with a laugh like a horse and an open, friendly manner.

"No, no. This is the perfect branch," Garvey insisted. "See how it catches the light here?"

Loraine bent and plucked a sterling silver sled from one of the baskets. "Then I'll just hang this on that branch. Perfect, don't you think, Kathy?"

"Well, I—"

"The sled's all wrong for that branch," Garvey pronounced. "What do you think, William?" he asked, turning to a gentleman on his left. "You own the largest engineering company in the state. There must be some sort of efficient system we could use here in determining what goes where."

Loraine leaned toward Kathy and said loudly, "One of Garvey's computer companies has just gone public and he's obsessed with efficiency."

William viewed the tree from several angles through narrowed eyes. "I think we should use a mathematical equation, employing the sum total of ornaments, the square footage of the tree, and the number, length, and breadth of the branches. In that way we could divide the tree into sectors, and—"

"I think we should sort the ornaments out by size," a newcomer to the group volunteered. Kathy had seen his picture many times in the paper. He was Harold Ford, one of Dallas's leading movers and shakers, and president of one of the down-town banks. "Then we could put—"

Marissa came up behind Kathy, took her arm, and guided her away from the extremely serious discussion at the tree. "Come on, Kathy, let's leave the tree-decorating to these very capable people. There's someone who wants to say hello."

"Where's Paul?" Kathy asked as they threaded their way around groups of people. She'd been so fascinated by the fact that anyone could actually decorate a tree through a mathematical equation, she'd failed to notice she hadn't seen Paul for quite some time.

"He's sitting down over there."

Kathy followed the direction of Marissa's nod toward a corner of the room where she saw Paul lounging in a large chair. Several people were sitting around him, talking to him. "Is his arm bothering him?"

"I don't think so. I imagine he just got tired of the throng."

"Maybe I should go check on him."

"Don't worry about him. He's fine." Marissa brought her to a halt in front of a couple, the female half of which was very pregnant.

The young woman smiled and stuck out her hand. "Hi. We've met, but we haven't been formally introduced. I'm Beth Ann Markovich, and this"—she indicated the tall, earnest, nice-looking man beside her—"is my husband, Drake."

"Of course!" Kathy nodded to Drake and took Beth Ann's hand to shake it. "Paul's assistant. It's nice to see you again."

Beth Ann grinned. "I thought I'd run into you at your apartment, but we've been missing each other."

"I've enjoyed all the food you've either cooked or brought from restaurants."

"Thank you, and I've been admiring the wreath above Marissa's fireplace. It's just beautiful, and she tells me that you helped her make it."

They all turned to gaze at the white marble

fireplace in which tiers of white votive candles flickered, giving the illusion of warmth without the heat. The wreath hung above the mantel. "Not really. I had nothing more than an advisory capacity on that project."

"Don't let her kid you," Marissa said. "Her tips were invaluable. I could have easily ended up like CeCe, with my fingernails glued together. Hi, CeCe." She waved at her friend, who was standing across the room, flirting outrageously with a very handsome man. CeCe waved back without missing a beat.

"All the materials came from your shop, right?" Beth Ann asked. "And from what I hear, you inspired her to try it."

Marissa nodded. "She did that. You'll have to visit her shop, Beth Ann."

"I want to. There might be some things I could make for the baby's room."

Her husband patted her arm. "And just when do you think you're going to have time to do all this? You're already putting in too many hours down at the office. I can't wait until your maternity leave starts."

Beth Ann made a face. "Drake is worried that I'm working too hard, but I'd go crazy just sitting at home, doing nothing but waiting for this baby to come!"

"So sit home and make things for the baby's room. One or the other, Beth Ann, not both."

Beth Ann's eyes shone with love as she gazed up at her husband. "Ah, my lord and master has spoken. Excuse us, we're going to go sample some of the wonderful delicacies you've laid out tonight, Marissa."

"But she's going to skip the champagne," Drake said sternly.

"Better skip the punch, too," Marissa advised. "Ask one of the waiters to get you a glass of milk."

"Good idea," Drake said.

Beth Ann groaned. "We'll see you later."

"I don't think I've ever seen two happier people," Kathy commented, watching Beth Ann and her husband stroll away, arm in arm.

The expression in Marissa's amethyst eyes turned dubious. "He looks like he'd like to wrap her in cotton and put her in a glass box until the baby comes. I don't think I could stand it!"

"You could if you were that much in love."

"No chance of that," Marissa said flatly.

Remembering what Paul had said about Marissa's brief marriage, Kathy bit her tongue to keep from saying anything more on the subject. "I was surprised to see Beth Ann here."

"Beth Ann is part of Paul's 'family,' so that makes her part of mine." Marissa smiled warmly at her. "And now, so are you."

Kathy's eyes widened in surprise. "That's very nice of you, but Paul and I . . . as soon as he's able, he'll be moving out of my apartment."

Marissa glanced over at Paul, a trace of concern knitting a line into her brows. "I hope you're wrong, Kathy. Paul needs someone like you."

"Me? I'm sure there are any number of Dallas women standing in line for Paul."

"Yes, but you're the first since Sarah that . . ."

Marissa gave a light laugh. "Never mind. Paul will kill me for talking to you like this. He and I have a deal. We're always there when the other needs support, but we never, but *never* meddle in each other's lives. Getting him to this party was the first time I've broken that deal. Oh look, you don't have anything to drink. Why don't you go over to the table and help yourself? I have to play hostess for a while."

Kathy cast another glance at Paul and found him laughing at something a very pretty young woman was saying. She headed toward the refreshment table filled with elegant finger food.

Waiters were passing among the partygoers with silver trays bearing fluted champagne glasses. Kathy decided to try the cranberry punch and discovered that it was potent enough to give her Connecticut Tea a run for its money.

"Isn't it good to see Paul here tonight?" asked a woman who was standing behind her.

"Yes, it is," a second feminine voice answered. "This is the first Christmas party I've ever seen him at."

"I know. Usually he's long gone by this time."

"The stabbing obviously delayed his plans this year."

"Only for a little while, I'm sure. I imagine he'll be leaving within the next few days, and I guess he'll be taking Kathy with him this year."

There was a laugh. "He's never taken the same woman twice, has he?"

A click of a tongue sounded. "I just don't understand why every year at this time he feels the need to go to the Caribbean."

"Well, my dear, it's because of Sarah, of course."

They moved off, and Kathy was left disturbed and bewildered. She felt like shouting, "What do you mean because of Sarah? *Sarah's dead!*"

Paul was withdrawn and silent on the way home. Trying not to be obvious, Kathy kept an eye on him. When they arrived at her apartment, he headed straight for the bedroom. She took hold of his arm, stopping him. "Are you in pain?"

He looked down at her hand on his arm. It was the first time since she'd helped him with his bath that she'd voluntarily touched him. "Not really." It was true. Marissa's party had extracted a toll from him, but not physically.

"Then would you like a cup of tea? I'm going to fix myself one."

"All right." His inclination was to go into the bedroom and be alone. But Kathy was actually volunteering to spend more time with him, and so he retraced his steps to the living area and settled into the big, overstuffed chair.

Resting his head against the back of the chair, he studied the little tree that Kathy had brought home. She had transformed it into something quite lovely, using a single strand of lights and an assortment of origami ornaments. Delicate angels, snowflakes, churches, candles, stars, and bells hung on the tree, each one a work of art in its own right.

She had made the ornaments late at night, after she thought he'd gone to sleep. But instead of sleeping, he'd lain in bed, missing her presence beside him, listening for her quiet movements in the next room. Each night he waited until she put aside the materials of her project, bedded down on the couch, and fell asleep. Only then did he shut his eyes and sleep.

"Here it is." Kathy handed him a cup of tea, then took a place on the sofa across from him.

He eyed her over the rim of the cup as he took his first sip of the hot, bracing liquid. He was tired of the constant strain, and wanted to try to rectify the rift between them. "You looked very beautiful tonight," he said softly. "Did you have a good time?"

She nodded. "Ummm. Marissa is a wonderful hostess."

"She's renowned for her parties. People campaign for her invitations, and if they don't get them, they consider their whole year ruined."

"That's hard for me to understand." She paused, trying to gather her thoughts. "There's also something else I don't understand."

Paul set his cup of tea aside. "What's that?"

"Since I've known you, I've heard several cryptic references to a trip everyone expects you to take. It seems a foregone conclusion with your friends. Tonight I overheard a conversation between two women about you."

His face took on a wary expression. "What did they say?"

"They said you'd probably be leaving within the next few days, and you'd be going to the Caribbean."

He made a vague gesture with his hand. "I've

been meaning to talk to you about that. It's true. I will be leaving soon, and I'd like you to go with me. In fact, I've already had Beth Ann make the reservations. I think you'll like it down there. The water's warm and so clear you can see right through a wave."

She stared at him. "I think you'd better explain."

He turned his head away. Then after a long moment, slowly, reluctantly it seemed, he looked back at her. "Every year for the past five years, I've left town at Christmastime to go down to the islands. That's why my friends view my trip as a foregone conclusion. First sign of Christmas and I'm gone."

"The woman said, 'because of Sarah.' "

"Sarah died on Christmas Eve five years ago. She was pregnant with our baby."

Something in her heart moved. "I'm sorry."

"She was so excited about Christmas. We were newlyweds and she was going to have a baby." He bent his head and rubbed his forehead hard, almost as if the memories inside were clamoring to get out and he didn't want them to. "She had decorated every inch of the house." He gave a hollow laugh. "I couldn't turn around without bumping into a reindeer or a Santa Claus. She was full of plans for our future and our baby's future."

"What happened?" she asked softly.

"The night before Christmas Eve I had to fly out to California. I was scheduled to be gone less than twenty-four hours. While she was sleeping, she suffered a cerebral hemorrhage and died. She and

Marissa had had a date to go shopping the next morning. Marissa came by to pick her up and got no answer. She called the police, and they broke in and found her."

"And you had to fly back to Texas knowing that your wife was dead. It must have been awful for you."

"I just kept thinking that I should have been with her."

"It would have happened even if you had been there." He shifted slightly in the chair, and she went on. "Marissa has told me what a wonderful woman Sarah was."

He nodded. "She was. Everyone loved her."

Kathy felt stricken. For Sarah. For Paul. For herself. *All this time there's been a ghost between us, and I haven't even known it.*

He continued, "She's been gone five years. I'm through grieving, but there's still this sorrow that increases at Christmastime when all the memories come rushing back." He leaned forward, his face earnest. "I solve the problem by going somewhere that doesn't remind me of Christmas."

Kathy raised her shoulders in a somewhat bewildered gesture. "But—"

"I need you to understand this, Kathy. The body braces for a blow it knows is coming. That's what I do. I *anticipate* and try to avoid the ache. It's so much easier that way."

Kathy understood. He hated Christmas because Sarah had died on Christmas Eve. He said he was through grieving, but he wasn't.

"Come with me, Kathy. I always rent the same house. It's really very charming, and—"

"Is that where you've taken the other women?"

He sat back and looked at her. "I told you there've been other women since my wife's death."

In an impatient move, she stood up. "It doesn't matter. I can't go with you."

"The shop's doing well now. It doesn't need your constant presence. I'll hire someone to look after it while we're gone."

"You don't understand, Paul. I don't *want* to go with you. See, I actually like Christmas, and I want to spend it here in Dallas, in my home."

She swirled around, picked up her tea, which had grown cold, and took it into the kitchen. She stuck the cup in the microwave oven and punched out one minute on the digital timer. She sensed Paul's presence behind her. "Strange things, microwaves," she said. "You can't see or smell them as you can a burning fire. They have no aesthetic value. They can't even keep you warm, yet people don't feel their kitchen is complete unless they have one."

"Can I stay here until I leave for the islands?" he asked quietly.

She went still. "Well, of course. You need looking after."

She felt his hand tangle in her hair. "No, I don't. I've been fine for some time now. My shoulder's still sore, but the wound is well on its way to healing."

She turned around to face him, pulling her hair through his fingers as she did. "But the sling?"

"It takes weight off my shoulder, giving me support, and I suppose it's not a bad idea as a precaution against some kind of new injury, but the truth is, I can go without it for a couple hours at a time now. I just haven't done so when you've been around, that's all."

She could have confessed a few things herself, she thought. Like the fact that she'd known he was getting better, but hadn't said anything because she didn't want him to leave.

"You didn't answer my question, Kathy. Can I stay?"

The palms of her hands had begun to sweat, yet she felt cold with nerves. "You remind me of a cat I had when I was a little girl. It was winter, and I saw him out in the snow. I brought him in to feed him and warm him up, intending to keep him for just a few days. The thing was, I just couldn't bring myself to put him back out in the cold." She wrapped her arms around her waist.

Paul shrugged out of the sling and tossed it aside. Gently, he put his hands on her shoulders. "Is that an answer?"

She stared across the kitchen, unable to look at him. "The funny thing about that cat was, he eventually left on his own. I guess he had his own timetable to go by, his own life to live, and he knew when he had to leave. I missed him when he left."

With a finger under her chin, he turned her face up to his. His eyes were as blue as she'd ever seen them, without a trace of gray. "Kathy, I'm sorry. I've got nothing to offer you. But I need you. *God*, how I need you!"

*And I love you*, she thought, but you still love

Sarah. She came away from the counter, pushing him aside and pacing back into the living area. Pausing in front of her little tree, she flicked at an intricately fashioned white dove.

She was proud of what she'd accomplished, she thought, with the tree, and the shop, and her life. The shop would continue to flourish. Next year she would have a new tree. But Paul would be gone.

She'd always known the two of them could never have any kind of future together. Whether it was the fault of the laws of nature or something else, she didn't know. But there wasn't anything she could do about it.

Kathy couldn't compete with a ghost. She wouldn't know how, even if she wanted to. When Paul left in a few days to fly to the Caribbean, it would be a victory for the past. When he left, he'd be rejecting the present. *He'd be rejecting Kathy.*

Suddenly, Kathy smiled to herself as she realized that, despite this painful knowledge, *she couldn't reject him first.* She'd give him everything she could until he left. And then it'd be over.

She didn't know whether she was being mature or stupid, but in the end, she supposed it didn't matter. Either way, the pain would be just as intense, the loss just as real.

She turned to find him standing not two feet away. "You can stay here until you leave for the islands. By the way, when are you leaving?"

"Christmas Eve, in the morning."

She nodded, accepting.

He went on, as if he felt the need to justify his actions. "I've never stayed this long into the season, but I've got to leave on Christmas Eve. I *can't* be here for Christmas Eve."

She understood. He was staying in Dallas as long as he could because of her. But there was only so much he would do for her.

He closed the distance between them. "Tonight . . . sleep beside me . . . in my arms."

She looked up at him, and a mass of lustrous red hair spilled down her back. "Yes. I will."

# Nine

In the bedroom, Kathy turned her back to Paul and pulled her hair to one side. He skimmed the zipper down to her waist, where he encountered the belt of ribbons. Its knots didn't deter him. In moments, he was tossing the satin lengths of pink, mauve, and soft fuchsia onto the bed. The dress came off just as easily and was soon a forgotten heap on the floor. His clothes made the heap higher.

Words would have gotten in the way. The only sounds were those of hands moving over heated skin. Breath being drawn in quickly, then let out slowly. Limbs sliding against limbs under the sheets.

Both Kathy and Paul were careful of his shoulder, but at the same time, they were aware that time was their enemy and the clock was relentless.

Between them there was such need. Lips discovered, mouths took charge, bodies caught fire. It was a night of complete surrender, yet each of them held back. Pain and sorrow receded, yet they remained at some distant level.

Surging together, Kathy and Paul became one. But only temporarily, because desire climbed . . . fire became hotter . . . passion crested.

And then, lovely and sweet, the waning carried them downwards, into the depths of the night where they held each other and slept.

Dawn's light had already begun to gently creep into the room when they awoke to find themselves entangled in satin ribbons.

Paul took the end of a pink ribbon and flicked it over her cheek.

She smiled without opening her eyes. "I'm surprised we didn't kick that belt off the bed sometime during the night."

"Did I tell you how beautiful you looked wearing this belt?"

Her eyelids slowly rose to see him propped up on his elbow, looking down at her. "No. At least not in detail."

"But my eyes must have told you what I was thinking. I was stunned."

"Thank you."

"And your hair . . ."

She chuckled. "All I did was put a few curlers in and my hair sort of exploded."

Lightly holding the belt, he trailed all ten ribbon ends across her throat and then down to the valley between her breasts. "Those long, loose, red curls made every man in the room want to comb his fingers into them."

Her brows arched skeptically. "You're making that up."

"I, for one, couldn't take my eyes off you." The ribbons were now tracing a path around each breast. "I couldn't stand it when you talked to another man."

Heat followed the trail that the ribbons were taking over her skin. "I didn't talk to very many men. On the other hand, every time I looked over at you, there was a woman doing her best to fascinate you with her many charms."

He made a loop of one ribbon and snagged the loop around an erect nipple. He grinned when he heard her indrawn breath. "I didn't notice anyone's charms but yours." Pulling in opposite directions on the ribbon, he tightened the loop around her. "Lord, Kathy, but it's so good to have you beside me again in this bed." And then his mouth closed over the nipple, ribbon and all.

She couldn't believe the sensations. Her breasts began to ache with renewed need. A fire started in the pit of her stomach and radiated downwards. And soon, she was writhing beneath him, unmindful of the brightening day, or the lengths of pink, mauve, and soft fuchsia twining around them and encasing them in satin.

"Please come with me to the Caribbean," Paul murmured. He was stretched out in bed, watching her dress for work. "I need you with me."

She turned and looked at him, allowing herself

to feel an incredible sadness for just a moment. Paul would make love to her, he would feed her, he would give her companionship, and he would take her to the Caribbean for Christmas. He would even stock her kitchen with an array of the very latest appliances. But that was *all* he could do. He couldn't love her.

"There are certain things I need, too, Paul. And escaping to the Caribbean for Christmas is not one of them."

He dropped his gaze to his hands, which were folded across his bare stomach. What could he say to that? He certainly couldn't blame her. "Since I'm leaving so late this year, I'll only be gone a week, two at the most. When I come back—"

"No."

At the quietly spoken word, he looked up. "Kathy, the trip won't change anything between us. I'll still want you, and you'll still want me."

"That's true."

"Then try to understand. I can't be in Dallas on Christmas Eve."

She whirled away from the mirror and faced him. "I do understand. Now you understand this. Once you leave, you can't come back to this apartment or to me. It'll be over between us."

He sat up, then grimaced because his sudden movement had caused a dull throb in his shoulder. She went to him and eased him back in an upright position against the pillows.

Strategically it was a bad move on her part, because he grabbed her arm when she would have moved away from him. "Make sense, Kathy."

"If you leave, the past will have won." She was

so close to him, she could see the anger flare in his eyes.

"It's just a simple, damn trip! It's not a question of anyone winning or losing!"

"If you leave, it proves that the past means more to you than the present."

"That's stupid!"

"I'm not asking anything of you, Paul."

"It sure sounds like you are."

She shook her head, pulled away from him, and stood up. "The lock on my front door opens easily—from the inside."

"Kathy—"

"Don't ask me to give up my pride, Paul."

After Kathy left for work, Paul lay where he was without moving for a long time, badly shaken, knowing that she had every right not to allow him back into her life when he returned to town.

She had given him all the love, sweetness, and generosity she was capable of sharing. And yet, he couldn't love her in return. He couldn't even bring himself to tell her the rest of his and Sarah's story.

He couldn't tell her that the reason he had married Sarah—the only reason—was that she'd been pregnant. He couldn't tell her that as wonderful as Sarah had been, and as much as he'd wanted their baby, he hadn't been able to love her as she had loved him. He had tried, though, and he had hoped that with time the genuine affection he felt for her would turn to love. But in terms of love he had failed Sarah. And he'd failed her again when she'd had to die alone.

• • •

Kathy stared out the front window of her shop. The sky was overcast, but all day the temperature had been in the high fifties. The extended weather forecast offered no predictions of snow for Christmas. Kathy had resigned herself. On that special day, she wouldn't have snow . . . nor would she have Paul.

Christmas Eve was tomorrow. Robert had packed two bags for Paul, and they were standing ready by her front door.

Their time together had been very precious to her, but at the same time, very hard on her. His presence had filled her apartment. Signs of him were everywhere. The scent of his cologne permeated the fibers of her sheets and drifted on the air in the bathroom. Remote controls to various stereos and televisions lurked beneath covers, under the bed, and on tables, waiting until they were needed and discovered again. His silk pajama bottoms never seemed to find their way into a drawer, but lay over a chair or in a pile on the floor, creating a glossy pool of color.

Everything would leave with him, but she knew vivid images would linger—the way he crinkled his toes when he saw an action sequence on television, as if somehow he was helping the protagonist by using body language. And the way he was constantly making sure that she ate. And the way he could make her body come alive beneath his hands.

She had done her best to block out the stark reality that, after tomorrow, she would never see Paul again. And she had paid a price for the effort. Her emotions were brittle; her nerves were shot. Loss of control was coming. She could feel it. She only prayed that by the time she fell apart, Paul would be gone.

It was nearly time to close the shop, and it was getting dark outside when Kathy saw Charlene Carelli pull her BMW into a parking space in front of the shop and jump out. Charlene had been in the shop several times, and Kathy had helped her with various projects, finding her an eager and adept student.

Charlene was breathless by the time she got inside. "You've got to help me, Kathy!"

"What's wrong?"

"I have a first-class emergency on my hands, and I've got no one to blame but myself. I waited until the last minute to order my centerpiece for a dinner party I'm giving tonight, and because of all the holiday parties, it seems every florist in town has run out of poinsettias. Can you help me?"

"Well, sure. We can put together an arrangement using silk flowers. It won't take too long."

"Oh, that's great." The relief in Charlene's voice was palpable.

Kathy set about gathering large white and red silk poinsettias, Styrofoam, and spools of red and gold ribbon. Together the two women managed to create a centerpiece worthy of any dinner table.

Charlene stood back and viewed the finished product. "Kathy, I can't thank you enough."

"No problem. You said you had silver candle holders and taper candles?"

Charlene nodded.

"Put them on either end of the arrangement, then."

"I will." The sale had already been rung up and paid for, and Charlene picked up the centerpiece, preparing to leave. "Thanks again. It was a fortunate day for all of us when Paul called Marissa and asked her to organize all her friends to come into your shop. You're just wonderful! Most of us had no idea making things ourselves could be so much fun."

Charlene had nearly reached the door when Kathy found her voice. "Wait a minute!"

With one hand on the door and the other balancing the arrangement, Charlene looked back over her shoulder. "Yes?"

"You mean all the people who have been coming in here know Paul, and they know each other?"

Charlene looked puzzled at Kathy's strident tone. "Well, goodness! Between Paul and Marissa, they know a lot of people!"

"And the only reason all of you have been coming in here is because you were doing Paul a favor?"

"Kathy, we didn't even know your little shop was here! But now that we do, you can bet we'll be frequenting it. Along with a lot of others." She opened the door. "I can't wait to hear the compliments on my centerpiece. I'll see you after the holidays."

The door shut behind Charlene. Kathy was left alone. And the thing that she'd been fearing finally happened. She lost control.

As she stood there, she could almost feel her nerves unraveling, as a hot anger began to climb.

Rational thought became an impossibility. Only action made sense.

As quickly as possible, she closed the shop and headed her bicycle toward Paul's office, where he had told her that he and Beth Ann would be working a little late to make sure everything was done before he left tomorrow. Night had fallen, dropping the temperature. Traffic seemed particularly heavy. She had no idea how long it took her to pedal the miles. She wasn't even aware when a light mist began to fall.

On the nearly deserted thirty-fifth floor of the Hayes Building, lights still burned. Kathy's progress to Paul's office was unhampered by the protective secretaries and receptionists that had made her first visit difficult, and she was able to walk straight in.

Paul was sitting behind his desk, his head bent over papers. Beth Ann had her chair pulled up beside his and was taking notes.

The scene registered in Kathy's mind only fleetingly. "We need to talk," she said.

Paul's head jerked up in surprise. "Kathy, what are you doing here? How'd you get here?"

"We need to talk," she said again.

He rose and started toward her. "Well, sure, but you're wet! Beth Ann, get a couple of those towels from the bathroom."

As befitted a woman nine months pregnant, Beth Ann stood slowly and carefully, then disappeared in the direction of the kitchen with a slow, awkward, swaying gait.

Paul pressed a kiss to Kathy's lips. "You're cold. Come sit down." He tried to pull her toward the couch, but she bolted away from him. "Kathy, what's wrong? Has something happened?"

"Yes." She hadn't known that her skin was cold, but she was frustratingly aware that the words she wanted to say to him had frozen inside her.

Beth Ann came back with a stack of terry cloth hand towels. "Here you go, Kathy. Dry off real well. It's so easy to catch a chill this time of year."

"Thank you." She took the towels and held them to her chest.

"If you want to get out of those clothes, Paul keeps several shirts and things in the closet in his private bathroom. There may even be a bathrobe. And there's a shower. Steaming hot water might feel good."

She managed a smile for Beth Ann. "Thanks, but I'll be fine. It's only a light mist. I didn't get that wet."

Beth Ann placed a hand at the arch of her back and made a slight grimace. "Paul, I'll be at my desk when you need me. I think I'll start on those memos."

"Fine." His eyes were on Kathy. As soon as Beth Ann was out of the room, he said, "Okay, tell me. What's wrong?"

Words thawed and came flooding out. "I just found out that you had Marissa ask all of her friends to come into my shop and buy something. That's despicable!"

Paul wasn't in the best of moods, and his nerves were strung tight. With his flight leaving in the morning, he felt as if he was walking a razor's edge. He'd be destroyed if he stayed in town and faced Christmas. And he'd be destroyed if he left

Kathy and couldn't come back to her. Without wanting to, he lashed out. "Despicable? Your business has increased a thousand percent!"

"But because of *you!* Not because of anything *I* did!"

"What's the difference how it happened?" He tried for a conciliatory tone, but his emotions were running too high, and he failed. He reached for her and was surprised to find her trembling. She allowed him to hold her only for a few seconds before she abruptly broke away. "Kathy, you're not thinking clearly. The important thing is that now you're able to make ends meet."

"Sorry, I don't agree. I think the important thing here is that almost from the very beginning, you've manipulated me! You bought me groceries! You moved in with me—"

"Feeding and caring for someone is not a sin, Kathy. But dammit, pride is." He paused, willing away his tension. "Look at it this way. The Hayes Corporation planned to advertise the village, aiming at the upscale market and thereby bringing new business in. Remember? So just view what I did as early advertising."

"Except this wasn't a business act, was it?" Her brows were drawn together as she determinedly tried to maintain logical thought through the many layers of her anger. A slim thread of reason was telling her that only the top layer had to do with his interference in her life. But for the moment, the top layer was the strongest, and she went with it. "I remember when Marissa and CeCe first came in. They were the vanguard, weren't they? That meant you called Marissa right before you went to California." She didn't even wait for his confirmation, but rushed on. "Probably immediately after we had our argument that day in your office. I guess you figured your only alternative was to improve things at the shop so that I could afford the rent hike. And since you don't love me, the motive had to be your desire to get me back into bed with you."

Like a steel-tipped arrow finding its mark, the truth of her words pierced Paul's conscience. He couldn't deny what she was saying, so he took a different tack. "Everyone in the village has benefited from the increase in business, Kathy. It hasn't been just you."

"I'm happy for them, but the positive results don't make it any easier for me to bear the hidden motives. And I just came to tell you that I want you to have Robert pick up your bags. You can sleep at the hotel tonight."

"No!"

"What difference can it possibly make? You're leaving in the morning for the Caribbean, anyway. Christmas, remember? I've heard of people being afraid of the dark, and thunderstorms, and snakes, but never Christmas!" As soon as the words left her mouth, she realized that all the layers of her anger could be condensed and explained with one reason: *he was leaving her*.

Pale, Paul clenched his fist. "Tell me something, Kathy. If I had helped all the other tenants in the village and not you, would you be this angry? And if I'd left well enough alone and let you lose your shop and starve, would you be this angry?"

"No, of course not!"

"Then let me ask you one more question. When is pride a *virtue*, and when is it a *vice*?"

Every light in the office went out, and they were plunged into blackness.

For a moment Kathy was too stunned to speak. His words had hit her hard and were making her think.

In the dark, his hands reached for her. "Are you all right?"

"Yes. Is it just your office, do you think?"

"It's got to be a blackout. Look out the window. There're no lights anywhere."

"Oh, great. That's just great."

"Don't worry. We've got candles in the kitchen. But stay here for a minute while I go check on Beth Ann."

Just then they heard the door open. "Paul?"

"Don't move. Let me come to you."

"Paul," Beth Ann's voice wavered, "my water just broke. I'm in labor."

# Ten

"I can't be in labor!" Beth Ann said as Paul guided her toward the couch. "I'm not due for two weeks!"

"Have you tried explaining that to the baby?" Paul asked.

"My dialogue with my baby has been rather limited up to this point."

"I see. Well, here's the couch. Just sit down and take it easy."

"Take it easy? Are you serious?"

"I meant, relatively speaking."

While Paul and Beth Ann were talking, Kathy used her memory of the general layout of the office to find her way to Paul's desk where she patted around on its surface until she located the phone. "I'm going to call for an ambulance. Paul, you mentioned there were candles in the kitchen. We're going to need some light."

"Right." His voice came to her in the darkness,

strong and calm. "What else should I get while I'm in there?"

"Do you have any blankets? We should keep her warm."

"We've got tablecloths. Oh, and there are nice, big, thick towels in my bathroom."

"Good. Beth Ann, how long have you been in labor? The paramedics will want to know."

"I'm not sure. I've had a backache for a few hours now, and it's gotten steadily worse."

"For heavens sakes, why didn't you tell me?" Paul asked, his voice sounding farther away as he strode across the large office.

"Because I just thought it was a backache! If you'd ever been pregnant, Paul Garth, you'd know that pregnant women have lots of backaches. And don't yell at me! Ohhhh!" After a few moments of silence, she added, "And don't make me yell at you, because it hurts!"

Kathy heard Paul mutter something right before he opened the door at the far side of the room. Beth Ann sounded close to tears. Anxious to comfort the young woman, Kathy punched 911.

She quickly told the dispatcher what was happening. The news he gave her in return wasn't heartening. With the blackout, the number of heart attacks and accidents had climbed. He took the information, though, and promised to dispatch assistance as soon as possible. The last thing the man said to her was, "You realize that the elevators won't work until the power comes back on. Since you're on the thirty-fifth floor, it's going to be quite a while before the paramedics can reach you, even if you're next on their list."

Kathy tried to keep her voice as even as possible. "I see. Okay, well, thank you. We'll wait for the ambulance. And in the meantime, if we have any questions, I'll call you back." She hung up the phone and began to feel her way toward Beth Ann, talking as she went. "Everything's going to be fine. They know you're up here and will come as soon as they can. In the meantime, you're not to worry about a thing."

"Kathy, I can't have this baby now!"

"I know you'd rather wait until you're in the hospital, but since your water broke, you may not have much choice."

"No, you don't understand! Drake's out of town, and I refuse to have this baby until he comes back!"

Kathy realized that panic was rapidly replacing the tears in Beth Ann's voice. She finally reached the couch, and knelt close to Beth Ann. "Where exactly is Drake?"

"Houston."

"We'll call him. He can get on the next plane home. First babies take a long time. That flight's only about forty-five minutes. He could be here before the baby arrives." She didn't believe a word of what she was saying, but, she decided, comforting Beth Ann was more important than being honest. And it worked.

"Good." Beth Ann's tone was heavy with relief. "That's settled then. I'll just wait for my husband."

The flame from a candle flickered brightly as Paul walked back to them. "I got all the candles and candleholders I could find, plus as many tablecloths as I could carry. I'll go back for the rest as soon as we get these candles lit."

"Paul, you don't have to worry," Beth Ann said. "Kathy's going to call Drake, and I'm going to wait until he gets here to have the baby."

"Can you do that?"

"Of course I can."

Beth Ann reeled off a phone number to Kathy, and while Paul stuck candles in the holders and lit them, Kathy went to make the call.

Five minutes later, she hung up on the father-to-be, who, she predicted to herself, would reach full-scale hysteria before his plane was airborne. Guided by the soft glow of candles, she returned to Paul and Beth Ann.

"Drake'll be here as soon as he can," she told Beth Ann. "He said to tell you he loves you very much and to be brave."

Apparently, Drake had said the wrong thing.

"Oh, sure! Easy for him to say! He's two hundred and fifty miles away . . . surrounded by women who all have flat stomachs! He ought to be *here*. Ohhhh!" Suddenly Beth Ann clutched her huge abdomen. "Lord, but this isn't fun!"

"Have you taken natural childbirth classes?"

Beth Ann nodded.

"Good, then you know a certain amount of procedure."

Beth Ann shook her head. "I can't remember a thing! Drake is supposed to be my coach. He's supposed to remember. He's supposed to be *here!*"

Paul spoke up. "Beth Ann, do you think you'd be all right alone for a couple of minutes while

Kathy helps me gather up a few other things in the kitchen?"

"I don't see why not. I'm certainly not going anywhere."

Paul sent Kathy a meaningful glance and picked up two of the candles. She nodded. "Beth Ann, just yell if you need us."

"You can count on it."

In the kitchen, Paul turned to Kathy. "How much trouble are we in?"

"If there are no complications with the birth, we should be fine. And if things do take a turn for the worse, we can call nine one one."

His mouth tightened with worry. "Always assuming we'd have the time to call. If anything happens to either Beth Ann or that baby . . . I shouldn't have had her up here, working this late. I should have thought!"

She put her hand on his arm. "Hey! We're going to manage just fine. After all, babies are born every day." Kathy was trying to sound calm, but in reality she was scared to death. And she was finding it incredibly touching that Paul, a man who was always so in charge of things, was as frightened as she was.

"But if anything goes wrong—"

"Paul, we'll do everything in our power to see that it doesn't. Okay?"

He covered her hand with his and squeezed. "I'm so glad you're here with me!"

"I am, too." For an all too brief, precious moment, she allowed herself the pleasure of softening just slightly against him, then she forced herself to straighten and return to the matter at hand. "Is this a gas stove?"

"Yes, thank goodness." He bent to open a cabinet door and pulled out a pan. "I can boil water in this. By the way, in the movies, *why* do they always send the man off to boil water?"

"I think it's to get the man out of the scene for a while so the heroine can have a few minutes of glory. In our case, though, common sense tells me we're going to need sterilized water to wash both the baby and the mother. Let it come to a rolling boil, then bring it in. Oh, and bring some of these towels with you. I'd better get back to Beth Ann." She picked up one of the candles and turned, but he stopped her.

"Kathy?"

She threw an inquiring glance at him over her shoulder.

"I . . ." He paused, appearing to search for words. "I'm glad you're here," he said at last.

Since he'd said that before, Kathy wasn't sure how to respond. The words *I love you* were right on the tip of her tongue, but she had told him that once and received a painful lesson. It wasn't love that he wanted from her. Thankfully something else flashed into her mind. "Garbage bags! I hope you have some."

Silently, he produced a roll of plastic bags and handed them to her.

"Great." A momentary pang of love made her wish that she could stay with Paul in this cozy little kitchen. Then reason reasserted itself. "I'll see you back in there."

Beth Ann's face was pinched with pain when Kathy sank down beside her on the couch.

"Wouldn't you know my kid would want to do things his own way? If you ask me, this doesn't bode well for our future parent-child relationship."

Kathy smiled. "I predict you're going to be a great mom. I envy you."

"You do?"

"Sure. You're about to have a Christmas baby, and Christmas babies are very precious and special."

"That's true, isn't it?" Beth Ann said, right before another contraction gripped her.

"I think it's time we got ready for the little one here." Seeing the alarm on Beth Ann's face, she added, "Just in case."

Kathy pulled all the cushions off the couch and arranged them on the floor. Then she laid garbage bags over the cushions, and spread two of the tablecloths over that.

When Paul returned, he helped Kathy move Beth Ann onto the makeshift bed. Kathy undressed Beth Ann and covered her well with tablecloths and towels, for both modesty and warmth. Paul placed a tray nearby on which he had put the now cooling pot of water.

Beth Ann might have been in pain, but it wasn't stopping her from talking. "This is not a good idea!" she said. "Who thought of this?"

"Now's a hell of a time to be asking that," Paul said, squatting down beside her and taking her hand.

"Now I remember whose idea it was! It was my *mother's!* 'I want a grandchild,' she said. 'Every one of my friends has grandchildren,' she said. *Shoot!* I just should have bought her one!"

Kathy couldn't help but grin, but there was no humor in her voice when she murmured, "The contractions are getting intense."

"What can I do?" Paul asked.

"Tear some of these tablecloths into strips." A sudden thought hit her. "You know, I've never been in an office before that has a complete supply of tablecloths and candles."

The remark had been addressed to Paul, but Beth Ann in her talkative mood never gave him a chance to open his mouth. "Paul gives a lot of business breakfasts, lunches, and dinners. We have four complete sets of china, and we have two sets of sterling silver, plus—" A groan halted her rapid inventory.

Kathy placed her hand over Beth Ann's stomach. "You're too tense. You've got to relax. Otherwise, you're not going to be able to take the pain."

"I know. You're right. You're absolutely right. I've got to . . . calm down now and start . . . thinking of my baby. He'll be here soon. Or . . . she will be." With great effort, Beth Ann deliberately slowed and deepened her breathing, inhaling through her nose, exhaling through her mouth.

Time passed quickly with Kathy and Paul intent on making Beth Ann as comfortable as possible. When the pains worsened and began coming closer together, Beth Ann rose to the occasion. She found one spot, on one corner of a gold picture frame, where a tiny glimmer was being reflected from one of the many candles in the room, and she focused on it.

Kathy took up position between Beth Ann's legs, and Paul held her hand and whispered words of encouragement. Occasionally he wiped off her forehead.

"I can see the baby's head!" Kathy suddenly cried out excitedly. "Next contraction, push!"

Beth Ann did, and with the next contraction, Kathy was holding the head in her hand. "Wonderful!" Kathy dipped one of the strips of cloth into the sterilized water and gently cleaned out the baby's mouth. A moment later, the baby let out a squall.

Paul laughed. "That's Beth Ann's baby, all right. I'd recognize that noise anywhere."

"I'll get you for that," Beth Ann whispered between exhausted gasps.

"Just a few more pushes," Kathy encouraged.

When the little shoulders came out, Kathy grasped them and gently pulled, and all of a sudden, the baby slipped out and into her hands. She gave a cry of delight. "Beth Ann! It's a boy! A beautiful little boy!"

"Really? Oh, Lord, is he all right?"

"He's perfect." Kathy glanced at Paul and knew a moment of surprise. It could have been a trick of the candlelight, but she could have sworn that she saw the gleam of tears in his eyes. Then he turned his head away, and she went back to her work.

She lifted the baby and placed him on his mother's stomach. He was wailing something awful, and Kathy could feel reaction threatening in herself. But she knew that to falter now would be disaster. She'd just have to wait until later to fall apart.

With hands that showed a slight, but nevertheless surprising tremor, Paul wrapped the baby in a tablecloth, then handed him to his mother. Beth Ann eagerly pulled her baby to her breast. The cries quieted. The adults heaved a collective sigh of relief.

Kathy sat back for a minute and allowed herself to enjoy the miracle. Surreptitiously she eyed Paul. She could see no sign of tears now, but he was strangely pensive and silent. She supposed his reaction was normal. After all, they'd just been through an enormously intense and moving experience. She knew that she'd never forget it for as long as she lived.

She'd told Beth Ann the truth. She did envy her. To be able to give birth to the child of the man she loved was something for which a secret part of her had always yearned. But now she knew it was never to be.

"I'd better clean you up, Beth Ann," she said, reaching for more strips of cloth.

When she finished, Kathy looked up at the new mother. The expression on Beth Ann's face was filled with more peace and love than she'd ever seen on one person.

"Thank you, Kathy," Beth Ann murmured, gazing down at her baby. "And, Paul, you were great. Now you'll know what to do when your wife has a baby."

Through the candlelight, Paul and Kathy's eyes met and clung. Then the lights came back on.

• • •

Paul gazed through the nursery window and watched as the nurse placed Beth Ann's baby in an incubator. The hospital personnel had assured Paul that this was standard procedure, and that the baby was in excellent condition.

Paul still couldn't believe everything that had happened. He and Kathy, surrounded by darkness, had helped to bring a new life into the world! It had been a beautiful, wondrous experience. And then the lights had come on and the paramedics had arrived. It had been decided that Paul would ride with Beth Ann in the ambulance to the hospital, and Kathy would stay behind to clean up and to call the airport, leaving a message for Drake to go directly to the hospital. Drake was with Beth Ann now.

Paul briefly wished for Kathy to be here with him. They'd worked in such harmony, sharing the experience of the birth with Beth Ann, that it didn't seem right that she wasn't here to share this moment, too.

But maybe it was for the best, he decided. He had a lot to think about. As he stared down at the squirming, tiny, red baby, he realized he'd never been so aware of the continuing process of life. Birth and death. Death and birth.

Five years ago, his baby had died before it had ever had a chance to be born. He hadn't been there for either the baby or for Sarah. And all this time, the strength of his pain and guilt had bound him to the past and blinded him to what was right before his eyes, in the present. But witnessing the miracle of this birth had somehow helped him face certain realities that he hadn't been able to see.

He'd wanted his baby with all his heart, and he'd tried very hard to love Sarah. But if he hadn't been able to love her, he'd cared for her a great deal. And Sarah hadn't been unhappy. She'd loved her life with him and had had a strong belief that some day Paul would love her.

Even if he'd been in bed beside her that night, he wouldn't have been able to save her. The doctors had told him that at the time. And his loving her wouldn't have saved her, either. He'd just never let himself believe it before now.

Tonight, though, he'd finally realized the truth. Life was a wonderful, precious gift. Because of his guilt, he had been avoiding life . . . and love.

If he'd lost a baby, he'd also brought one into the world. Nothing could ever replace the baby he'd lost, but in some crazy way, the birth of this baby had shown him the way to his second chance. He could bring more babies into the world, only these babies could be his. His and Kathy's.

He'd put Kathy through so much. He had so much to make up to her, and he had a lot to tell her. He just prayed she'd let him.

"What do you think, Paul? Is my son Heisman Trophy material or what?"

Paul wasn't at all surprised to see a beaming smile plastered over Drake's face. "He definitely is. You're going to have to hire someone full time to handle the colleges that are going to be beating down your doors to get this kid. How's Beth Ann?"

"When I left her, she was compiling lists of names. You should know that the name Paul is featuring prominently in a lot of them. I told her I don't care. The only thing that's important to me is that both she and the baby are okay."

Paul looked back at the baby who was currently screaming at the top of his lungs. "Well, they're both certainly that."

"Thanks to you." Drake took Paul's hand in his and pumped it vigorously. "I can't tell you how much I appreciate what you and Kathy did. *Wait a minute!* My son shouldn't be crying like that." He tapped on the window. "Nurse, nurse!"

Used to nervous new fathers, the nurse smiled at him reassuringly and then proceeded to ignore him.

"She can't hear what you're saying, Drake. That window is soundproof."

"Nurse!" He tapped on the window again, this time harder. "Don't let my son cry! Pick him up! Give him a toy! Wait a minute!" He gave Paul a wide-eyed look. "He doesn't have any toys! We've got to go buy him some toys!"

Paul was hard pressed not to laugh. "It's eleven o'clock at night. All the toy shops are closed by now."

"Then we've got to get them to open up!" He grabbed Paul by the hand and started pulling him down the corridor. "Come on!"

This time Paul let his laughter come out. Yes, he thought, life was indeed precious and joyous. And some unsuspecting toyshop owner was in for a big shock.

The day of Christmas Eve was sunny and mild, and almost from the time she arrived at the shop, Kathy was kept busy. Christmas Eve, it seemed, brought out panic in people—panic over things they hadn't done yet and gifts they hadn't bought.

But Christmas Eve, she was finding, also brought out a very special gaiety and joy. Everyone seemed to have such purpose. They talked of the splendid dinners they were going to cook, or the loved ones they couldn't wait to see, or the surprises that were in store for their families.

Kathy listened to their stories, all the while trying to forget that Paul hadn't come back to her apartment the night before. And when the hands on the clock pointed out that it was ten-thirty, she tried not to think of his plane taking off, winging him toward the Caribbean.

At eleven, she called the hospital and was told that the mothers had their babies now and were nursing and couldn't take calls, but that, yes, Beth Ann and her son were doing very well.

At noon, she rang up a sale, wished the woman a happy holiday, and for the first time allowed herself to acknowledge that she was completely miserable. As the minutes ticked away, customers became a blur to her. When she finally discovered herself all alone, she couldn't even summon the energy to come out from behind the counter. She sat down on the stool and eyed the M & M's bowl. Even though the bowl had a plentiful supply of green M & M's, she decided against eating one. It wouldn't be the same. Nothing ever would. Her heart was lost to a man who, with every minute, was flying farther and farther away from her.

Her pride and Paul's past had been too much to overcome.

*What was she going to do without Paul in her life?*

The question still hung silently in the air around her when Paul walked into the store.

Shock and a guarded happiness stiffened her spine. "Did you miss your plane?"

"No," he said quietly, "but I nearly missed my life. The night I told you about Sarah—our marriage and her death—I left out something."

"What do you mean?" She sensed something different in his manner. His strong voice gave her hope, though she knew she shouldn't be feeling such an emotion. His intense gaze made her approach him, though she knew she shouldn't get too close.

Her feelings were registered on her face, and when she reached his side, he raised a hand to briefly touch her cheek. "My sweet, lovely Kathy." His words came out in a broken murmur—even he could hardly hear them—but he had so much that he wanted to tell her and his voice grew stronger as he went on. "I'm sure you felt that my grief and love for Sarah were keeping me from loving you. The truth is, I didn't love Sarah, and my guilt over that fact has stood in our way."

"You didn't love her?"

"Sarah's the only one who knew while she was alive. After her death, I told Marissa and James."

"But you married her!"

"She was pregnant. And she was such a truly wonderful and giving person, I believed I *should* love her. I was sure I would with time, but that time never came. She died without my loving her, and I felt so terrible about it that I put a stop to the most important thing in life."

"I don't understand."

"I'm not sure I do, either. But you see, I strongly believed that I had cheated Sarah because I couldn't love her. After her death, I was determined to do better. Ever since, in some weird way, I've felt that as long as I couldn't give my love to any other woman, I wouldn't be cheating Sarah. It doesn't make sense, does it? Yet my subconscious mind has been telling me all this time that it did."

"Oh, Paul." It did make sense, she thought. It was the way the human mind worked. It could turn in on itself and . . . bite.

He cupped her face with his hand. "And then you came along, and I felt all the things for you that I hadn't for Sarah. But, even though I wasn't aware of it, the barrier of my guilt intervened and I told myself I didn't and couldn't love you." For the first time since he'd entered the shop, he smiled. "I was so wrong."

Pure happiness flooded her veins, hitting her system like the most potent of narcotics, and she was rendered speechless.

"I knew that I wanted you with me all the time, and that I worried about you, and that I wanted to take care of you. I just didn't carry my reasoning to its logical conclusion. I love you, Kathy," he said, huskiness thickening his voice. "I love you so much. Please forgive me for all I've put you through."

"There's nothing to forgive. You're a good man with a hyperactive conscience who's been imposing a tremendous, unnecessary burden on yourself." She wrapped her arms around him and tilted her face up to his. "I love you. I've loved you almost from the beginning. But I haven't been without blame, either. If my idiotic pride hadn't kept getting in the way, maybe *I* could have seen things more clearly."

He hugged her to him. "Lord, Kathy, I never knew what happiness felt like until I met you."

"It's Christmas," she said tenderly. "A time of miracles."

A strange look passed over his face, and Kathy instantly wished she could recall her words. Was Christmas still a time of pain for him?

"Have you noticed?" he said softly, gazing down at her. "It's snowing."

"It's what?"

"It's snowing."

With a smile that seemed to grow bigger and bigger with each passing moment, he drew her to the window. She looked out and gasped. Every square inch of the village was covered with snow, and snowflakes were flying past the window.

She gave a laugh of elation. "Paul, it's snowing! I can't believe it. The sun is shining, and it's snowing! Isn't it wonderful? Come on, let's go see it!"

As she rushed to get out the door, Kathy marveled at the miracles that had taken place. Her shop was a success. It was Christmas Eve in Dallas, and it was snowing! And—to her, the biggest miracle of all—Paul loved her!

Once outside, she was greeted by a beautiful Texas day, canopied by an incredibly blue sky.

Confused, she glanced around, then started in surprise. Three huge snow machines were busily churning, covering the sun-filled village with a blanket of snow, and creating a glistening, magical winter wonderland.

People were crowding out onto the sidewalks from the shops, and drivers were stopping their cars in the street. Children squealed with delight and dived into the snow, while parents watched and laughed. Cameras were appearing from everywhere and pictures were being snapped, recording this amazing event.

Kathy looked up at Paul, tears making the green color of her eyes appear as dark and as brilliant as emeralds. "You did this for me!"

"Merry Christmas," he murmured, pulling her back into his arms.

## THE EDITOR'S CORNER

Have you been having fun with our **HOMETOWN HUNK CONTEST**? If not, hurry and join in the excitement by entering a gorgeous local man to be a LOVESWEPT cover hero. The deadline for entries is September 15, 1988, and contest rules are in the back of our books. Now, if you need some inspiration, we have six incredible hunks in our LOVESWEPTs this month . . . and you can dream about the six to come next month . . . to get you in the mood to discover one of your own.

First next month, there's Jake Kramer, "danger in the flesh," the fire fighter hero of new author Terry Lawrence's **WHERE THERE'S SMOKE, THERE'S FIRE,** LOVESWEPT #288. When Jennie Cisco sets eyes on Jake, she knows she's in deep trouble—not so much because of the fire he warns her is racing out of control toward her California retreat, as because of the man himself. He is one tough, yet tender, and decidedly sexy man . . . and Jennie isn't the least bit prepared for his steady and potent assault on her senses and her soul. A musician who can no longer perform, Jenny has secluded herself in the mountains. She fiercely resists Jake's advances . . . until she learns that it may be more terrifying to risk losing him than to risk loving him. A romance that blazes with passion!

Our next hunk-of-the-month, pediatrician Patrick Hunter, will make you laugh along with heroine Megan Murphy as he irresistibly attracts her in **THANKSGIVING,** LOVESWEPT #289, by Janet Evanovich. In this absolutely delightful romance set in Williamsburg, Virginia, at turkey time, Megan and Dr. Pat suddenly find themselves thrown together as the temporary parents of an abandoned baby. Wildly attracted to each

*(continued)*

other, both yearn to turn their "playing house" into the real thing, yet circumstances *and* Megan's past conspire to keep them apart . . . until she learns that only the doctor who kissed her breathless can heal her lonely heart. A love story as full of chuckles as it is replete with the thrills of falling in love.

Move over Crocodile Dundee, because we've got an Aussie hero to knock the socks off any woman! Brig McKay is a hell-raiser, to be sure, and one of the most devastatingly handsome men ever to cross the path of Deputy Sheriff Millie Surprise, in LOVESWEPT #290, **CAUGHT BY SURPRISE,** by Deborah Smith. Brig has to do some time in Millie's jail, and after getting to know the petite and feisty officer, he's determined to make it a life sentence! But in the past Millie proved to be too much for the men in her life to take, and she's sure she'll turn out to be an embarrassment to Brig. You'll delight in the rollicking, exciting, merry chase as Brig sets out to capture his lady for all time. A delight!

You met that good-looking devil Jared Loring this month, and next Joan Elliott Pickart gives you his own beguiling love story in **MAN OF THE NIGHT,** LOVESWEPT #291. Tabor O'Casey needed Jared's help to rescue her brother, who'd vanished on a mysterious mission, and so she'd called on this complicated and enigmatic man who'd befriended her father. Jared discovers he can refuse her nothing. Though falling as hard and fast for Tabor as she is falling for him, Jared suspects her feelings. And, even in the midst of desperate danger, Tabor must pit herself against the shadowed soul of this man and dare to prove him wrong about her love. A breathlessly beautiful romance!

Here is inspirational hunk #5: Stone Hamilton, one glorious green-eyed, broad-shouldered man and the hero of **TIME OUT,** LOVESWEPT #292, by Patt

*(continued)*

Bucheister. Never have two people been so mismatched as Stone and beautiful Whitney Grant. He's an efficiency expert; she doesn't even own a watch. He's supremely well-organized, call him Mr. Order; she's delightfully scattered, call her Miss Creativity. Each knows that something *has* to give as they are drawn inexorably into a love affair as hot as it is undeniable. Just how these two charming opposites come to resolve their conflicts will make for marvelous reading next month.

Would you believe charismatic, brawny, handsome, *and* rich? Well, that's just what hero Sam Garrett is! You'll relish his all-out efforts to capture the beautiful and winsome Max Strahan, in **WATER WITCH,** LOVESWEPT #293, by Jan Hudson. Hired to find water on a rocky Texas ranch, geologist Max doesn't want anyone to know her methods have nothing to do with science—and everything to do with the mystical talent of using a dowsing stick. Sam's totally pragmatic—except when it comes to loving Max, whose pride and independence are at war with her reckless desire for the man she fears will laugh at her "gift." Then magic, hot and sweet, takes over and sets this glorious romance to simmering! A must-read love story.

Enjoy all the hunks this month and every month!

Carolyn Nichols

Carolyn Nichols
Editor
*LOVESWEPT*
Bantam Books
666 Fifth Avenue
New York, NY 10103